TAINTED ASHES

UNTOLD TALES: CINDERELLA

LAURA GREENWOOD

Tanwyn has always known her station in life, especially with the Duchess ruling her life.

A chance encounter with the Prince changes everything, and Tanwyn finds herself having to foil a plot, with only the help of her dragon familiar, Dart, to do it.

Can she save the Prince by midnight?

-

Tainted Ashes is a fantasy retelling of Cinderella and part of the Untold Tales series. It can be read as a standalone.

CHAPTER ONE

Soot coated my face, no doubt streaked with sweat. I both loved and hated it when the Duchess assigned fire duty to me. There was something comforting about being faced with the slowly dying embers, then building them up for when the next day dawned once more. Fire burned away the bad things, and left what it didn't need behind. It was simple. And while wild, it was also predictable. At least, it was to me.

I checked over my shoulder to make sure no one else was in the kitchens. The whole night would pass before the cooks arrived to bake the morning bread, and I was going to make the most of it. I held my hand out in front of me and clicked. A tiny flame leapt up from my fingers, flickering and casting tiny shadows across the hearth.

Before I could even fully appreciate it, the flame died, and I was left in the dark of the kitchen once more. Disappointment flooded me. No matter what I did, the most I could produce was the tiniest of sparks. I wasn't sure what I needed to do to change that. Other than *something*. Probably have formal training with one of the realms magicians, but that wasn't going to happen. It would cost money, and if there was one thing the Duchess didn't like, it was her girls costing her money.

I jumped as I caught the ashes shifting in the grate from the corner of my eye.

"Dart," I scolded. "I've told you not to do that."

The tiny dragon popped her head from beneath the pile, the white ashes falling away from her dark scales. She shook her head, ridding herself of the rest of them, and then cocked it to the side, as if asking me why she shouldn't be playing in the remains of the fire.

"If you get caught, we'll both be in trouble," I whispered.

Dart shook her head.

"Fine. If you're caught, *I'll* get in trouble. Do you want that?"

She paused, then shook her head again.

"Good. I thought not."

Footsteps sounded from outside the kitchen, and my eyes widened. That isn't good.

"Quick, get back under there and I'll light the fire," I warned the dragon.

She chittered, but disappeared back under the ashes. I tried to spark my fingers, desperate for some kind of flame to catch onto the kindling I'd stacked there.

"Come on," I whispered, hoping it would coax out my magic.

The footsteps drew nearer. If they entered the room and realised Dart was in here, there'd be trouble to pay. And not just for me. Dragons were rare and prized creatures, and I didn't like to think about what might happen to Dart if I let them get hold of her. She'd probably be fattened up, then killed and sold for parts.

A shiver ran down my spine simply from thinking of it. How could people do that to such beautiful creatures?

I let out a sigh of relief as a spark finally flew from my fingers and into the kindling. The soft glow of flames cut through the wood. I leaned in and blew on it, encouraging it to grow hotter and more certain. Dart would be having the time of her life beneath the ashes. She loved it when the fire burned around her. I supposed it gave her some kind of strength she didn't normally have, or something like that. I didn't know much about dragon lore, and couldn't sneak into the library more often than once every couple of months. The Duchess never assigned me to the library, I wasn't sure why. Potentially because she knew I *could* read, while some of the other girls could not.

The door at the opposite end of the kitchen creaked open.

"Tanwyn? Is that you?" the familiar voice of Jill called out.

"Yes," I responded. "Just setting the fire so the cooks don't come in to a cold grate again." One of the girls had been beaten for that last week. Not by the cooks, they'd done everything they could to avoid it, but like everyone else in the castle, they were in thrall to the Duchess. She was the one who punished us all, no matter how high we were on the serving chain.

"You have to hurry, bed check will be happening in five minutes."

I tried not to roll my eyes. It was a habit I needed to break, especially as it wasn't a good one for a serving girl to have. "I have to set the fire, even if it means I'll be late."

"I know," Jill said. "That's why she sets those kinds

of tasks." She clasped her hand over her mouth, her eyes wide and frightened.

"I won't tell anyone you said that," I promised.

She shook her head. "It won't matter. She'll know, she always does."

There was no denying what the other girl was saying. No one knew how the Duchess heard whispers and secret conversations, but somehow, she always did.

"She might not this time," I assured my friend. "And there's nothing we can do if she has, other than wait."

Jill rushed forward and sat down beside me as I waited for the fire to grow bigger.

"You need to go to bed," I warned her. "If you don't, you'll get into trouble."

She shrugged. "If the Duchess heard me talking about how our chores are designed to keep us from bed for that reason, then I'm already there."

Despite myself, a chuckle escaped me. She had a point there. The Duchess was careful, and wouldn't be caught out doing the things she did, but we all knew she loved to punish us, and would come up with any reason to do it. But she liked to think of herself as a fair woman, which meant she had to have a *reason* to punish us. Apparently, her morals didn't stop her from manufacturing the slights.

The fire shifted and panic flooded through me. What was Dart up to? Couldn't she hear that I had company? I looked between the fire and Jill, horrified to find her staring at the flames. What would she do if she saw the dragon? She'd believe me if I told her Dart was my friend, but it would be dangerous knowledge all the same, especially when Jill had a punishment coming up. Nothing stayed secret in this castle for long, especially when more than one person knew about it.

"It's looking strong now," Jill said.

I nodded. "But I want to make sure. Why don't you go upstairs and I'll join you in a couple of minutes?" I suggested, mostly so I could ask Dart to look over the fire for me.

Jill pulled a face, but then nodded. "I'll try and stall the inspection if it starts before you get there," she promised.

"No, you won't. You shouldn't do anything else that might get you into trouble," I reminded her. "Slip into bed, and I promise I'll be up before the bell rings." I only needed a couple of moments' privacy to ask Dart for help, nothing more than that.

It only took her a moment to chase away the indecisiveness. She rushed off in the direction of the stairs, desperate not to get into trouble. It was a miracle we were all still alive if I was honest. So often it felt as if there was no point to it.

"Dart," I whispered hastily to the fire.

The little dragon popped her head up, framing herself in the flames. Her tongue darted out, as if trying to drink up the power they gave her. My heart melted a little at the sight. She loved the flames, I wished I could leave her in them more often.

"Will you watch over the fire for me?" I asked her. She nodded her head.

"Make sure you're gone before the cooks get here," I warned. "You don't know what they'll do if they catch you."

She gave an odd little yip that I'd always assumed meant she'd agreed with what I'd asked, but I had no real way of knowing.

"Good. I'll see you in the morning." I reached out and patted her head, ignoring the heat of the flames. The dragon wasn't the only one who could enter them untouched. Not that I'd ever tried anything other than my fingertips in the fire, I didn't want to be proven wrong.

I rose to my feet, giving one last lingering look at the grate. I didn't have time for this. The bell for inspection was going to go off at any moment, and if I was caught out of bed, I was going to be in serious trouble.

I rushed out of the door, taking the servant's stairs two at a time. I slowed when I was outside the door to our sleeping quarters, and slipped inside.

Jill motioned for me to hurry, and I went over to the empty bed next to her, slipping between the sheets fully dressed. I pulled the cap from my head and stuck it on the rickety wooden nightstand between us, before grabbing my nightgown. I should have put it on before getting into bed, but being caught fully dressed under the covers was preferable to being semi-disrobed out of them.

I squirmed around, pulling my skirt and stockings off, followed by my bodice. My underdress would have to stay on until the nightly bed check had been made, after that, I'd be able to take it off properly.

"You're going to get yourself into trouble one of these days," Jill whispered to me.

I smiled to cover up my unease. She had a point. "But not today."

"Girls," the Matron sang out as she walked into the room. She cracked a horsewhip against her bare hand. More than one person flinched. Most of the servants here felt the same way, we hated the way the Duchess treated us, but were helpless to do anything about it. But the Matron was different. It was almost like she enjoyed the power she wielded over us.

The woman's heavy step echoed as she walked up and down the room. I had no idea if everyone was even in their beds, if I was here well in advance of the bell, I'd always do a count, but this time, I hadn't been.

"Hmm. Everyone seems present today." She cracked the whip. "I hope everyone's chores have been completed. If not..."

The threat was left unfinished. We all knew what would happen if one of us hadn't done a good job.

The Matron didn't wait for any of us to answer, and swept out of the room, snuffing out the candles with a draft.

No one moved or spoke to one another. There was no point. Tomorrow would be another day as filled with work as this one had been, and we needed sleep in order to survive it.

CHAPTER TWO

"The Duchess is asking for you," Maria whispered
as she passed me on the stairs.

I grimaced. "Thank you." As much as I didn't
want to be called to wait upon the woman, it was
better to know she was expecting me and turn up
only a little after that. The alternative was to be
punished for being late, even if it wasn't my fault.
"Would you take this down to the laundry?" I asked,
lifting the basket of dirty bed linen I was holding so
she knew what I was talking about.

"Of course. You'd better get going." Maria took
the basket from me and began to hop down the
stairs. "Oh, and you might want to straighten your
cap," she said.

"Thanks," I muttered, and fixed it. I hated that she
was right and it had become unruly.

I half-ran up the rest of the stairs and down the corridor to the Duchess' room. I couldn't go any faster for fear she'd be able to tell when I stopped and berate me for being out of breath. That was yet another thing on the list of things the Duchess hated, and we were all here in order to make her life the easiest and most enjoyable possible.

I drew a calming breath and knocked on the door.

"Get in here," the Duchess barked.

I didn't need to be told twice, and pushed open the bedroom door, entering her private domain. The stench of overused perfume reached my nose. I pushed away the tickling sensation it caused and put a calm, and most definitely fake, smile on my face. She wasn't ever going to know she got to me.

"You asked for me, Your Grace," I said, dipping into a curtsy. I knew she'd be able to see me in the mirror, and it pleased her when we showed her the deference due to her station. Yet another thing we had to do for no reason other than her ego.

"I'm going out, and I need my hair doing."

I nodded, the reason why she'd called for me in particular becoming clear. For whatever reason, she'd decided I was the best when it came to teasing her curly blonde hair into something that could be seen as a reputable sign.

Silence filled the room as I pulled the pins from her hair and began to brush. If she wanted me to speak, or to get a musician in here, then she'd tell me. I'd long since learned not to ask her anything before she was ready.

I ran my hand under her hair, smoothing the way for the brush so it didn't tug on any particularly nasty tangles.

"I think an updo would be the best today," she said.

"Of course, Your Grace." I didn't curtsy this time, she wouldn't like it while I had hold of her hair.

My hands worked without much instruction from me, I'd done this so many times that it was barely necessary. Instead, my gaze roamed over the dressing table to see what had changed since the last time I was in here. This had become an odd game of mine I'd started as a way to test my memory.

Without meaning them to, my hands stilled as I caught sight of an official-looking invitation. The moment I realised what I'd done, I resumed work on the Duchess' hair, teasing it into a respectable bun so I could add the ornamentation she was fond of.

"You can ask your question," the Duchess said with a heavy sigh.

I paused for a moment, unsure if this was a trap, or if it was safe to actually ask. "I was just wondering," I started, my voice wavering ever so slightly. "What you'd been invited to, Your Grace. If I know, perhaps I could start thinking about ways to style your hair, if it would please you." The lie tripped off my tongue easier than I expected it to. I didn't care in the slightest what her hair would look like on the date in question. She'd no doubt rip apart any suggestion I had.

"Hmm." She didn't say anything else.

I knew better than to prompt her into a response. She either wanted me to know, or she didn't, all I could do was wait.

"I suppose it is better if you know, that way you and the other girls will know to be on your best behaviour." The Duchess sighed loudly, as if it pained her to be so kind to us serving girls.

I raised an eyebrow without thinking about it, then smoothed my expression out again. I looked down at her hair, wrapping one strand around another and using a pin to stop it coming undone.

"The Prince is coming to stay here. Just for the night. Matron will have all the instructions for you girls, so don't think you'll be getting off lightly," she warned.

Wait, the Prince? He barely ever visited his nobility this far out from the capitol. Perhaps it was too long a journey, or more likely, they were all as unlikeable as the Duchess and he was saving his sanity instead.

"I'll expect the lot of you to be on your best behaviour, of course."

"Naturally, Your Grace." I stepped back and dipped into a curtsy. "I'm finished, if you like it," I added.

She picked up a handheld mirror and used it to get a good view of the back of her hair.

"Adequate, but you should practice your skills more on the other girls," she instructed.

"Of course, Your Grace." I wanted to point out that I didn't have the *time* to practice on the other girls, we were all so busy with our chores, and the little time we could find for ourselves was over so quickly it wasn't even worth mentioning.

"Very good. I'll expect tea when I return at four. Inform the cook."

"Of course, Your Grace," I repeated, already annoyed at how many times I'd had to say those words since arriving in her chambers.

She swept out of the room, not even sparing a glance in my direction. I was fine with that. It was easier to be unseen in this house.

I listened for her footsteps to fade, then started

clearing up the pins and other items. The Duchess didn't like being able to hear when we were doing things like that. I was almost done when my gaze rested on the invitation again. Though I supposed it wasn't an invite, but some kind of proclamation. I wasn't sure how that worked.

With a quick glance over my shoulder to check no one was watching me, I picked it up and read the words. Learning to read was one of the dim memories I had of my childhood, before I came here at seven.

His Majesty, Prince Raynor requests residence at your castle in three days time.

Huh. There wasn't anything particularly interesting about the note. If anything, it didn't hold enough information about the impending royal visit. Was someone playing a cruel joke on the Duchess? I hoped not. We were the ones who would pay the price if that was the case, and I didn't want that for anyone.

Footsteps shuffled along the corridor outside. I hastily put the invitation back in its place and hurried out of the room. I still had all my chores left to do, attending on the Duchess simply took time away from doing them, rather than meaning someone else was assigned the task. This was a thankless world the woman had created within her castle.

I sighed and resigned myself to another day working with no end in sight. That was my lot in life, and I needed to stop dreaming of a better one. Nothing was going to change.

CHAPTER THREE

THE ROOM WAS FILLED with the flurry of dresses being chosen and the chatter of excited serving girls. What I couldn't work out was *why*. I longed to be in the kitchens or the stables with Dart, rather than here with the other girls.

"Aren't you going to pick one?" Julia asked me, twirling around with a horrendous pink gown pressed against her. Did she think it would look good on her? I wasn't sure, and I felt it was better not to ask at this point.

"I will." But only because I had to. The Matron had barged into our room today and announced that we were to get ready for the Prince's visit. I thought that would mean double the amount of chores and cleaning, but apparently, that wasn't the case. She'd left us here with the vague instructions of getting ready.

Julia danced away to talk to Nancy. Not for the first time, I felt as if I didn't belong with the girls here. Tanwyn wasn't a common name, and it certainly wasn't one that was used for the class of people who typically became servants. It was a noble name, and as a child, I'd heard the girls whispering about that and wondering where I came from. I tried not to think about it too much. What did it matter that I wasn't from one of the villages around here? Perhaps I was the daughter of a noble, one who'd owed the Duchess. To me, that made sense, even if it wasn't particularly *fair*. Then again, none of the girls here were treated fairly. Every day, everything was about how much the Duchess and the Matron could get out of them. It was all work, no play. And as far as I knew, I wasn't the only one who didn't get paid either.

"Have you seen this one, Tanwyn?" Jill called from across the room.

I looked over to the girl who'd become my best friend through nothing more than circumstance. She was holding up a soft blue gown which flowed in a straight skirt down. It wasn't as fancy as some of the others.

Knowing that I had to get ready along with the

others or I'd be in trouble, I made my over to her. I slipped the fabric of the dress through my fingers.

"It's beautiful," I said.

"And perfect for you," Jill said, pushing it into my arms.

"No, you should wear it..."

She shook her head, cutting off my protest. "I have a different one." She gestured to a stunning emerald gown behind her. "It'll bring out my eyes."

"It will," I admitted.

Her dress was fancier than the one she'd chosen for me, but not as ridiculous as the ones I could see the others getting into. Ten girls who wanted to be women all dressed in fluff and skirts with huge ruffles and puffed sleeves. Thankfully not all on the same dress, that truly would be a horrendous sight, and not one anyone would want to see.

"Why are we getting dressed up?" I whispered to Jill, not trusting any of the others with my question. They'd wave it away and tell me it didn't matter so long as they didn't do any work.

Jilly shrugged. "The Prince is coming."

"Hmm." That didn't seem like enough of an explanation. What did the Prince care what the serving girls wore? We were nothing more than the servants who kept the house running to him, nor should we be. That was how the system worked. The royalty ran the country through the nobility, and the rest of us served them and made it seem as if their houses cleaned themselves and food magically made its way to the table. It was a flawed system, that much was for certain, but one that did work on some level.

I ignored the chatter and slipped the dress on over the soft and silky undergarments the Matron had given us. Unlike the dresses, which I suspected had once belonged to the Duchess herself, the underskirts and chemise had been new. I loved the feel of them against my skin, even if they made me wary about what was to come.

"Will you button me up?" I asked Jill once I was mostly dressed.

"Only if you'll do my hair for me," she teased.

"Of course, I will," I promised, already thinking about the best way to frame her face with her beautiful red curls.

"Turn." She spun a finger around to mimic the movement.

Her deft fingers had my gown fastened in a matter of seconds. She was wasted on the chores she was given. Jill should be embroidering fine fabrics and showing off the beautiful things she could create. Just one more thing to add to the list of reasons why the Duchess' system didn't make the most of the resources she had.

"My turn," she said, and claimed a seat in front of one of the dressing tables in the room.

I smiled and made my way over to her. I released her hair from her cap and let the curls bounce down to her shoulders. It shone in the light, beautiful and captivating.

"Maybe we should leave it like this," I said. "Then you can captivate the Prince with a look."

She giggled. "I doubt I would. My nose is too crooked."

"It is not," I protested, even though she's right, her nose is a little crooked, but I thought it made her all the more beautiful.

"It's fine," she dismissed. "With hair this colour, my nose is normally overlooked anyway."

I didn't answer, and simply focused on doing her hair instead. I wanted to leave it mostly loose, it was too beautiful not to, but then I'd pin bits of it back and tease out some strands at the front to frame her face. I could see it all in front of me. By the time we were finished, no one would know she wasn't noble by birth.

The other girls were all dressed now and doing the same as we were. It was easier to do someone else's hair than our own. Nancy even pinched her cheeks and bit her lips to put some colour into them. I didn't see the point when it would fade within a few minutes anyway, but I supposed it also didn't hurt.

"There you go, all done," I said to Jill.

She jumped up, her eyes shining with excitement. "Do you want me to do anything for you?" she asked.

I shook my head. "I'm just going to put it back up a bun."

Jill frowned. "Don't you want something more special?"

"Not until I know what we're doing," I said. "I don't want hair getting in my eyes if I'm cleaning the floors."

"You don't think they're going to make us do that, do you? Not in these gowns." She shuddered, as if the idea of working while wearing something pretty was the worst thing imaginable. I supposed in some ways it was. There was a reason the nobility didn't do the hard labour of the lower classes.

One of the other girls caught her attention and she wandered off to start comparing the dresses they'd chosen. I watched in the mirror as an amused smile lifted the corners of my lips. I wasn't sure what was going on, and if I was honest, I was a little worried about it, but it had filled a room of silent withdrawn workers with laughter, and for that, I was grateful.

I let my hair down, then brushed it back into a

neat looking bun. A sparkle of blue on the dressing table caught my eye. I leaned forward and picked it up. A hair barrette, with stones a similar colour to my dress. I could make use of that. I slipped it into my hair, admiring how good it looked against the slicked-back blonde strands. I hadn't planned on adding any decoration like that, but now I had, I knew it was right.

"Attention girls," the Matron called. I'd been too distracted to hear her come in. I needed to be more careful about that. "If you'd all line up and follow me, the Duchess is waiting downstairs to talk to you all."

The others exchanged glances, and I could tell they wanted to talk to one another about what might be happening, but didn't dare because of the Matron. I stayed completely still, dread settling inside me. The Duchess hadn't talked to us all together in years, so whatever this could be, it wasn't good.

The girls started to follow her out of the room and down the stairs. I scraped my chair back and joined the back of the queue behind Jill. At least I'd be next to my best friend for whatever came next.

CHAPTER FOUR

WE LINED up at the bottom of the stairs, a rainbow of colours in our silk, satin, and damask clothing. It was richer than any of us had ever worn before, and I could tell from the way the other girls were shuffling about that they were starting to get uncomfortable. I'd have to thank Jill later for picking me a comfortable dress. It seemed as if that was the way she'd gone for herself too, as she stood completely still, not moving a muscle. I narrowed my eyes. Something was up with that. Why would she be so laid back while wearing a fancier dress than normal? Was there something she hadn't told me about where she'd come from?

I didn't dwell on that, it wasn't worth it. Instead, I watched as the rest of the servants filed into the room, standing on the opposite side of the staircase from us girls. The Matron went to stand with them. All of them looked smart, as if they were wearing the best clothes they owned, but none of their outfits came anywhere close to the extravagance me and the other serving girls had on. I tried not to think about what that meant, it only served to make me more uneasy.

We stood in silence, nobody moving or saying anything as we all waited for the Duchess. With no clock in the entrance hall, it was impossible to tell how much time had passed, and it felt like an age despite the fact it probably wasn't. If we'd had hours before she needed us, then the Duchess would have us working them.

The woman in question stepped into the hall a moment later. Her dress was a deep purple, a bold choice with royalty visiting, but she was a Duchess, and could get away with the choice, especially if there wasn't a royal woman arriving with the Prince.

"Good morning, everyone," she said loudly. "I've called you here to lay down a few ground rules for while His Majesty is visiting us."

One of the cooks leaned in to whisper something to a gardener. My gaze flitted to the Duchess, wondering if she'd seen the gesture, but she didn't seem to care in the slightest.

"You are not to be seen unless you are called for.

The castle must be spotless. There will not be anything out of place," she said, pacing back and forth. "If you are called for, you are to come immediately, no matter what you are doing."

I wasn't sure why she was telling us any of this. It all sounded like nothing more than a normal day under her rule.

"For today only, the girls are not to perform any of their normal tasks. But I expect them still to be done." She glowered at the other servants, who pulled faces as if they wanted to protest, but dared not. I didn't blame them. If they had to do all of their own work, and all of ours, they wouldn't get any sleep tonight.

But no one spoke. There was no point. What the Duchess wanted, the Duchess got. It was as simple as that and no one argued if they knew what was good for them. And we did. We'd had a lot of practice and experience with it.

"Excuse me, Your Grace?" Nancy asked.

I sucked in a breath, as did several of the other servants.

The Duchess' attention swivelled to her, an eyebrow raised as if asking her why she dared speak at all. "Yes?"

"If we're not to do our chores, then what would you like us to do, Your Grace?" she asked.

It was a valid question, even if it was a dangerous one to ask. I wasn't sure I'd have had the courage to.

"You will be diverting yourselves with reading, music, and walks in the garden," the Duchess answered.

My eyes widened. Why was this happening? It didn't make any sense.

"But I don't want to see any of you, and expect you to vacate any room I enter," she added.

I almost laughed. I didn't want to be in a room with her if I could help it anyway, having an excuse to leave any she walked into was a good thing as far as I was concerned.

"And if the Prince calls for you, you are to do anything he asks for." She paused for dramatic effect. "*Anything.*"

Confusion crossed some of the girls' faces, but I understood what the Duchess was getting at. The reason we were supposed to do all of those things was so that we could appear desirable to the Prince. If he called for one of us at night, then we were supposed to go. I wasn't sure if the Duchess wanted that so he would be pleased, or so she could use the information against him at a later date. I didn't think I wanted to know.

I felt sorry for the Prince. The Duchess tended to have beautiful serving girls, and I was certain he would find at least one of us attractive, though whether or not he'd ask for a companion remained to be seen. I'd never heard any rumours about the man being a womaniser, but then, I barely left the Duchess' castle, so what did I know.

"And if he does call on you, then as soon as he is done, you are to report to the Matron and tell her exactly what occurred," the Duchess ordered.

My stomach twisted into a knot. Was she really saying this? She wanted us to entrap the Prince and give in to his every whim, but at the end of it, report back to her so she could use the information.

I wasn't the only one who didn't seem to like the new development, a couple of the other girls were fidgeting noticeably, not wanting to go ahead with the things she was saying. I could understand that.

"He will be arriving any moment, please assume your places throughout the castle. And remember what has been said to you," she warned. "I don't want to see you in my way. You are expected to constantly be on the lookout for the good of this household."

I stopped myself from pulling a face at that. What good did any of this do us? We were all going to be trapped in basic slavery to her. If she did well, there'd be more of us, and more to do. Nothing was going to change.

"Dismissed," she said, walking off and leaving us to do what we wished.

Without thinking twice about it, I left the room and made my way to the stables. If I was going to have free time while the Prince was here, I was going to make the most of it and spend it with Dart. No one would bother me out with the horses, especially if the grooms and gardeners were putting in extra hours doing the work that one of us girls would normally do.

CHAPTER FIVE

I SWUNG my legs back and forth, enjoying the cool air against my bare skin. I knew I shouldn't have hiked my skirts up to my waist and sat like this, but it was hard not to when I'd been given such rare freedom.

Dart zipped past me with a soft whooshing sound.

I chuckled to myself. The small dragon was also enjoying her newfound freedom. Normally, she spent her days hiding from the people in the stables or the kitchens, and didn't spend it flying like she should. Deep down, I knew I should tell her to fly off and live her life away from me, but I couldn't do it. She meant too much to me. In a way, she was the only thing that kept me sane while living in this house, and I wasn't ready to give up on that yet.

As if she knew I was thinking about her, Dart landed next to me on the wall and cocked her head to the side, looking up at me for permission to do something. Probably climb on me if I knew her.

"Go on, then," I said, amusement creeping into my words.

She chirped, then lifted herself up in the air and landed on my shoulder. Her claws tickled my skin, but didn't hurt. She knew what she was doing when she sat there.

I reached up a hand and stroked her. She closed her eyes and made a soft clicking sound, almost like the purrs the kitchen cat made when it had eaten a particularly satisfying meal and then found the best spot in front of the fire.

Instead of saying anything, I closed my eyes and enjoyed the warmth of the slowly setting sun. None of the other girls had bothered me here, nor did I expect them to. No doubt they were enjoying the maze in the gardens, or the comfortable seats in the library. In other words, they were doing all the things we weren't normally allowed to.

"Excuse me?" a man asked from behind me.

I jumped, not having expected anyone to want to talk to me. Especially since I didn't recognise the voice. He was probably someone who came with the

Prince. I got up and turned around, dipping into a shallow curtsy. I had no idea who the man was, but I did know it was better to be polite. I tried to ignore the tickling sensation of Dart running down my back and disappearing behind the wall. At least she doesn't *want* to get caught, it makes protecting her easier.

"Can I help you?" I asked, making sure to keep my voice light and airy. The last thing I want to do is insult one of the Prince's retinue.

"It's a lovely sunset," he observed. "I was looking for somewhere to enjoy it, but I see this one is occupied."

"You can join me, if you want," I suggested. "I'm not doing anything interesting, but if you want to look..." I shrugged.

"Why would you want me to do that?" he asked, his brow furrowing.

What did he mean? "Aren't you angling for an invite?"

He chuckled. "Are you offering one?"

"It makes no difference to me if you sit next to me in silence, or if you go on your way. I'm only here for the peace."

"In which case, I shall take you up on your offer." He came around and perched himself on the wall next to where I'd been sitting.

I hopped back up, keeping my skirts over my legs this time.

"Are you enjoying your time here?" I asked after a few moments of silence.

"I thought you wanted to sit in peace," he teased.

"It felt rude to do that," I muttered.

He chuckled. "I understand that. It's one of the reasons I came out here in the first place. It seems as if no matter what room I go into, girls are constantly wanting to talk to me."

"Oh, they've been told to do that," I answered flippantly. "Sort of."

"Oh?"

I sighed, unsure if I should tell the man what was going on. It went against what the Duchess had said, particularly as he'd run back to his master and tell him what was happening. Then again, the Prince probably deserved to know what was happening so he could choose to avoid everyone if he wanted to.

"We've all been told to be as nice as possible to your master in case he wants to use us for *nightly pursuits*."

"My master?" the man checked.

"The Prince?" I countered. "I'm sorry, I haven't seen you before, I assumed you came with His Highness. Didn't you?"

"Oh I did," he said, an odd tone to his voice. "Nightly pursuits? Really?"

I nodded. "Between you and me, I think the Duchess wants us to spy on him, though who knows what she'd do with the information." I tried not to roll my eyes. This whole situation was ridiculous. Why was this even happening?

"I don't think the Prince will even be thinking about those."

Despite myself, I laughed, even though I knew I probably shouldn't. "I honestly didn't think he would be. I'm sure he has far more important things on his mind."

"He also respects his people, and would never treat a woman that badly," the man said.

"I like that." I stared out into the night, trying to work out where Dart disappeared to. I knew it was a good thing she wasn't still with me and gaining attention from the stranger, but I still missed her.

"Tell me, what else do you like about the Prince?" he asked.

"I see you're spying for him," I teased.

"I promise, I'm not."

I sighed loudly. "Honestly, I don't know anything about him, other than his name. We're not given many privileges here, so we don't hear about the world outside our walls."

"But you're all dressed so finely," he observed.

"We're not usually," I admitted. "It's normally rags and muck for us here. This is the first day off we've had since...well, I'm not even sure."

"It's that bad?"

"You get used to it," I admitted softly. "It doesn't sound good, I know..."

"It sounds awful. Have you tried appealing to someone?"

A short bark of a laugh slipped out of me. "Who is going to listen to me? I'm a serving girl. I don't normally wear silk and lace, I normally spend my days sweeping ash out of the grate and trying not to burn my hands." I held them up to show him the welts there.

The man sucked in a breath, then reached out. His touch was light, which was the only thing that stopped me from pulling my hands away. Why was he doing this?

"This is what working does for you?"

I shook my head. "That's what working every hour of the day does to me," I corrected. "I suspect a lighter workload and some time off to heal would avoid it."

"The Duchess does this to you?"

I nod.

"And she orders you to men's beds?"

"Oh, no. This is the first time she's done that, and I think it's just because it's the Prince. Not that it makes that any better. He doesn't deserve having spies forced on him."

"How do you know that if you've never heard anything good about him?"

I shrugged. "I've also never heard anything bad about him. And bad gossip always travels faster."

He laughed. "You have a point there."

A bell rang within the house, startling me into focus. I pulled my hands out of his, missing their touch almost instantly. I pushed the longing for more away. I shouldn't forget my place simply because a man showed me kindness. That was a good way to end up on the wrong side of everyone.

"I have to get going," I said. "That was the dinner bell."

He nodded. "I'll have to as well."

"Will you..." I trailed off, not wanting to voice the question on the tip of my tongue.

"Will I?" he prompted.

"Will you be at the servants' dinner?" I asked.

A sad look crossed his eyes. "Unfortunately, I must dine with the Duchess."

"But only the Prince is dining with her." Even as I said the words, understanding dawned on me. He *was* the Prince. "I...I'm so sorry, Your Highness, I didn't realise..."

"It's all right," he assured me.

I dipped into the deepest curtsy I could manage. "But I've been addressing you without using your title." And complaining about my station in life. I'd messed this up more badly than I could have ever imagined possible.

"Please, I'm not offended," the Prince said. "You admitted to not knowing anything about me, I should have been fair and told you then."

I straightened my back, the urge to ask him why he *hadn't* revealed his identity on the tip of my tongue.

"Because you looked so peaceful out here, and I didn't want to scare you away with who I was."

"How..."

He chuckled. "It was written all over your face," he responded.

"I should have recognised you, Your Highness." I hated grovelling, but for the Prince, I'd do it.

He grimaced. "Please don't call me that. Everyone else does, I have enough of it from them."

My brows knitted together in confusion, and I began to fiddle with the soft silk of my dress. "What would you like me to call you?" I asked, biting back the urge to call him an even more flowery name to get my point across.

"In public, Your Highness is fine," he admitted with a disgusted look. "But if we're alone, why don't you call me Raynor?"

I gasped. "By your name?"

"Whyever not?"

"It's not proper," I responded.

"Neither is engaging a lady in conversation without revealing my identity," he pointed out. "Yet I did it all the same. And I owe you a debt. Now I know I should watch myself around all of the ladies in the house save one."

"The Duchess?" I guessed.

A smirk lifted the left side of his mouth. "You," he pointed out.

"Oh."

"Would you be so kind as to let me know your name?"

My eyes widened. How had I not thought to introduce myself before now? "Tanwyn," I answered.

"A noble name."

"I don't know," I admitted. "I came here when I was barely old enough to remember everything."

"My Father's former Chief Advisor had a daughter named Tanwyn. She must be about your age now. Did you know Duke Floren?"

I shook my head. "The only member of the nobility I've ever met is the Duchess."

"That you remember."

"True," I admitted. "I've always assumed I was the daughter of some minor nobleman who got on the Duchess' bad side. Most of the girls here are to pay some kind of debt, from my understanding of the situation."

"The Duchess sounds charming," the Prin-Raynor, quipped.

"You'll never meet a more generous woman," I sent back.

"In which case, I shall ensure I keep my eyes on her throughout dinner," he said.

"You should."

"I wish you could join us," he said softly.

"The Duchess would never dream of allowing it."

"Perhaps you could accompany her to the ball I'm throwing next week?" he asked.

The second bell rang from inside, reminding me that I couldn't spend the entire evening out here talking to the Prince.

"I have to go," I said. "I can't be late or they'll ask where I was." I started to make my way back to the castle.

He reached out and caught my wrist gently. "Why don't you tell them you were with me?"

"Then they'll ask what we talked about, and I'd rather not betray your privacy like that."

"Thank you," he whispered. "I truly am humbled by that."

A blush spread over my cheeks.

"Will you try and get her to agree to take you to the ball?"

"No promises," I said softly. "But I'll do whatever I can to see you there."

"I'll be watching for you," he vowed.

And I for you, I thought as I ran back to the house.

CHAPTER SIX

I TRIED NOT to let my nerves show, but the tray I was carrying bounced up and down in my hands. The Duchess had asked me to wait on her and the Prince for breakfast, despite allegedly not wanting to see any of us. I wasn't sure what to do with that. Other than my job.

Dart rushed out from a crack in the wall beside me.

"Now isn't a good time," I told her in a hushed tone.

She shook her head and then gestured towards the door.

"You can't go inside." If she did, it would be a disaster. "The Duchess could see you."

The dragon didn't listen to me, I wasn't sure why I thought she would.

A Page stepped up next to me just as Dart disappeared back into the crack. Hopefully, she'd stay there and wouldn't cause any trouble. Even as I thought that, I knew it wasn't going to be the case. Dart had something planned. Or something had caught her eye, I wasn't sure.

The Page swung the door open for me. "Good luck," he muttered under his breath.

I shouldn't be surprised by his words, every one of the servants in this house would want to avoid this job. There was so much potential for things to go wrong.

The long table was already laden with dishes, probably the cold ones that the cooks could have laid out before the Prince and the Duchess got here.

The Prin-no, Raynor, looked up from his dish, a slow smile spreading across his face. No. That wasn't good.

I gave him the tiniest shake of my head. If he acted like he was interested in me, then the Duchess would stop at nothing until I was spying on him. And while I didn't want to betray his trust, I'd have to at least tell her something to get her to stop.

His gaze dropped back to the cold cuts on his plate.

I dipped into a curtsy to the Duchess first, knowing she wouldn't like it if I greeted the Prince before her, even if I technically should, given his superior position in the hierarchy of noble life. I'd never understand how the nobility worked.

"Your Grace, Your Highness, I've brought freshly poached eggs from the kitchens, if you wish for them."

The Duchess waved me away.

"I would, please," Raynor said.

My blood raced at the sound of his voice. I didn't realise how much of an impact our one conversation had on me, but now I knew I wanted to spend more time with him, and get to know him better. I pushed the thought away. It would get me nowhere. I was little more than a slave, and he was the heir to the throne. He didn't have time for someone like me, and nor should he. I would simply be a distraction from the kinds of people he should be socialising with.

I placed two of the eggs on his plate, then dipped into another curtsy.

"Is there anything else I can get for you?" I asked.

"Leave," the Duchess said, anger filling her voice. I didn't understand that. She'd asked for me to be here, why was it a problem now? The Duchess was a woman I'd never understand, even if I tried to.

"Actually, I'd like some more coffee, if that's all right," Raynor said, his eyes on me.

I nodded. "Of course, Your Highness." I set the tray on the table, and turned around.

My eyes widened as I spotted Dart running out from under the table. What was she doing here? She could get us into so much trouble if she was caught.

I stepped forward, trying to ignore the dragon and focus on my task. I knew Raynor only wanted the coffee so I'd stay in the room longer, but that didn't change the fact I had to make it.

The moment I went to move again, Dart got under my feet. I wobbled and then began to fall.

The scrape of a chair sounded, and Raynor rushed forward, catching me before I could hit the ground and then righting me.

"Are you all right?" he asked, alarm on his face.

I nodded. "Thank you," I whispered.

"Thank you, *Your Highness*," the Duchess said, her voice bellowing across the room.

Oh no. I'd forgotten she was there. Somehow.

I stood up properly and took in the sight of the formidable woman coming towards me, anger etched onto her face.

"I'm sorry, Your Grace, I tripped." I dipped into a curtsy, unsure if that would be enough to placate her. Knowing her, probably not.

"You should be paying more attention when you're in my presence," she fumed.

Interesting there was no mention of the Prince also being here. Which only drew my attention to Raynor's hands still being on my arms. A small part of me wanted to relax into him, but I knew that wouldn't be deemed acceptable.

"I'm sorry, Your Grace," I repeated. "It won't happen again."

"You're right it won't. Leave the room and send one of the others to replace you." She turned away.

"Your Grace, I don't think that's necessary," Raynor said, stepping away from me and into her line of sight.

My eyes widened. What was he doing? Didn't he know this would only make it worse for both of us? The Duchess didn't want anyone protecting her girls from her.

"As she is a member of my staff, I believe it is up to me to decide what is necessary," the Duchess said flatly, retaking her seat at the table and opening a paper, not paying attention to either of us any longer. I expected this dismissal of me, but it surprised me she would treat the heir to the throne with the same amount of contempt.

Raynor opened his mouth to speak.

I leaned in and placed a gentle hand on his arm.

He craned his neck so he could see me properly.

"Not worth it," I mouthed.

His expression darkened, and he looked between the two of us, trying to work out what he should do.

With a quick glance at the Duchess to make sure she wasn't paying any attention, I leaned in so I could whisper in his ear. "Anything you say will only make it worse for us all. The Duchess doesn't like being told what to do, even by someone who has the right to do it."

Understanding crossed his eyes. He didn't like what I was saying, but he recognised the need to heed my warning. He was already getting himself into a strong position for when he became king, and it wouldn't work if he didn't read the people in his kingdom correctly. The Duchess was a woman who needed to think she was in control, and to retain her obedience, he had to play into that.

"Thank you, though," I added in a whisper.

"You're welcome, Tanwyn."

A shiver ran down my spine at the way he said my name.

"I'll send Jill in a moment, Your Grace," I said to the Duchess.

She didn't even acknowledge I'd spoken. That was fine by me, I didn't expect her to.

I turned to Raynor and dipped down into a low curtsy, but met his gaze with my own. I wasn't sure *how* I knew, but he wanted me to feel like I was his equal, and even though I was currently showing him the respect owed to someone in his position, I wanted him to know I understood the message.

His lips twisted into a smile. Good. He understood me.

I left the room with a smile on my face, despite the dangerous interruption from my dragon friend. I wondered what she was up to. Whatever it was, it was a risk to us all, and I wasn't likely to ever get an answer about why she'd done it.

At least the Prince had proved himself to be as kind as he had been last night. There was always going to be a chance that he didn't act the same in front of people of his own social status, but I was glad to have discovered that wasn't the case. Whether the Duchess liked it or not, I was already more loyal to him than to her.

A small amount of kindness goes a long way, and she'd never given any.

CHAPTER SEVEN

I STRAIGHTENED the skirt of my faded and worn servant's dress, hoping Raynor wouldn't mind seeing me in it. With the Prince leaving within the next hour, the Duchess had removed our access to the fine dresses and put all of us back to work.

Except me. Though I had no doubt I'd be sent there any moment. But first, the Prince had asked to see me. Alone.

I swallowed down my nerves and pushed open the door to the room he was using. I hoped he realised the Duchess would have someone listening in the whole time. Or that she expected me to fill her in on everything he said to me.

"You came," Raynor said, true relief filling his voice.

Despite my apprehension, a smile spread over my lips. "Of course, I can't very well ignore a Prince, can I?"

He chuckled. "I'd expect you to ignore anyone you don't think worth your time."

"In which case, I wouldn't talk to a great many people," I teased. "But you would be one of the exceptions."

"I'm glad to hear it. Will you take a seat?" He gestured to one of the chairs. The light from the fire illuminated the fine weave of the fabric, and the intricate look of the embroidery. This wasn't the kind of seat I was normally called upon to sit on.

But he was expecting me to. I swallowed loudly, then sat down, trying not to worry about leaving dirt behind. My dress was clean, even if it was an old one.

"I see the fancy dresses have gone," he observed.

I laughed softly. "Long gone. Never to be seen again, unless you visit in the future, though even then I'm not so sure."

"Because I didn't engage any of you in conversation?" he mused.

I shuffled uncomfortably. "I'm going to be expected to report back on this," I said softly. "What would you like me to say?"

"Anything you want to."

"That's not going to cut it." And the last thing I wanted was to get the Prince into trouble, Raynor had been too kind to me for that.

"Perhaps say that I was merely enquiring after your health, that fall wasn't a natural one, after all."

I glanced away, trying to avoid him seeing the guilt on my face. The fall *hadn't* been an accident. Dart knew what she was doing, even if I didn't understand what motivations a tiny dragon could have.

"Well?" he prompted. "Do you think that will pass the examination you're going to receive?"

I shot him a bemused smile. "No. But if I stick to it, there's nothing anyone can do except call me an idiot for not talking about more important things."

"Maybe you should also mention the ball I'm having, and that I'd like you to attend."

"The Duchess will never allow that," I pointed out.

"Maybe not. But if she thinks it'll get on my good side, you never know what she might do."

I chuckled. "That's true." I wasn't going to pretend I understood anything about how the Duchess' mind worked. She was a mystery to us all.

"I hope you do come," he said, reaching out and placing a hand over mine. "I'd like to see you again."

"I'd like that too," I admitted. "But I'm not sure it'll be possible. The Duchess..."

"Is a piece of work, I'm aware of that."

I cocked my head to the side. "Is that why you came here? To see what she was like?"

"Partly." He shrugged. "But there's also been talk of unrest in the Lord Daryll's lands, and I needed to ensure she would protect the good of the kingdom."

"Do you think she will?" I asked.

"The honest answer is that I don't know."

"Why are you telling me that?" I blurted. "How do you know I won't run to her and tell her all of this?"

"Will you?"

I shook my head. "Of course not, but you don't know that for sure. I could be anyone. I could be tricking all of this out of you, I could..."

He picked up my hand and clasped it between both of his. "But you won't. I'm an excellent judge of character."

Despite my apprehension on the matter, a small giggle escaped. "I was never going to." How was he bringing out this side of me? I wasn't normally like this. Actually, that was unfair. I'd never spent this much time alone with a man, this could be completely me.

A knock sounded at the door. Raynor dropped my hands as we both turned to look.

One of the Prince's servants stepped into the room. "Your carriage is ready for you, Your Highness."

"Thank you, Vlad," Raynor responded. "I'll be there momentarily."

"I'll let them know." Vlad dipped into a bow and shut the door behind him as he left.

Raynor sighed deeply and turned back to me. "I'm afraid this is where we must say goodbye, Tanwyn."

"Unfortunately so." I didn't know what else I could say.

He lifted one of my hands to his mouth and placed a kiss there. "Until we meet again."

"That might not happen," I blurted.

"Oh, it shall. Even if I have to return for a visit to make it happen..."

"And put up with the Duchess fawning all over you," I quipped.

"I'd deal with a dozen Duchesses for you."

"You don't even know me," I pointed out. "We've had two conversations." And a lot of unacted on glances, but I kept that observation to myself. There was a chance he hadn't felt the same level of connection as I had.

"I'm an excellent judge of character, remember?" Mischief twinkled in his eyes.

"Then I look forward to the moment we meet again." It was strange to be saying things like this. Like we were characters in a children's tale and not two people trapped in the world where they had no control.

He swept into a low bow, causing my heart to skip a beat. No one had ever shown me such an act of respect before, and I wasn't too sure how to deal with it. Before I had time to decide, he swept out of the room, leaving me behind.

I turned around and stared into the flickering fire of the grate. I clicked my fingers, hoping one of the sparks would appear. A second later, a flame danced above my fingers. A reminder that, even if he wished it was different, I wasn't suitable for a Prince.

The door slammed and I whirled around, extinguishing the flame in my hand as I did.

"What did he want?" the Duchess demanded.

"To say goodbye," I answered honestly.

"That would have taken seconds," she sneered. "What else did he talk about?"

"T-the ball that's coming up." That was what he'd told me to tell her, in the hopes she'd bring me with her.

Her face scrunched up in disbelief, though the expression changed to one of disgust moments later. She didn't believe that someone like Raynor would be interested in someone like me, and that could work to my advantage. So long as I could convince her he'd thought of me as nothing more than a plaything.

"You weren't called to his bed," she observed. It isn't a question, and I didn't treat it like that. "So, what did you do?"

"I don't know," I admitted. "We only talked for a few moments, and it was only about the sunset."

"Useless girl," she admonished. "Go find Matron, she has a list of work for you to complete."

I wanted to ask why she was punishing me when I'd done nothing but talk to the Prince a couple of times, but I knew it was pointless. This was precisely *because* I'd talked to him, and he'd taken a liking to me. But not one she could use as blackmail down the line.

"Of course, Your Grace," I said, and dipped into the best curtsy I could manage given how much my entire body was shaking.

I didn't wait for her to dismiss me, this whole conversation had been one of those.

"I don't want to see you around the castle." A thread of jealousy spun its way through the Duchess' words. She wasn't as unaffected by the situation as she wanted to pretend, that much was clear.

I slipped through the door without answering.

Extra chores were preferable to spending more time in the Duchess' presence.

CHAPTER EIGHT

Dᴀʀᴛ ᴄʟᴜɴɢ ᴛᴏ ᴍʏ sʜᴏᴜʟᴅᴇʀ, swaying back and forth as I left the kitchens and head out to the vegetable patches by the East Wing of the castle. One of my extra chores was to put a circle of the ash around the patch to deter pests from eating the vegetables. Normally, we left the ashes in a box by the gardeners' shed, but this is punishment for me.

If I was honest, I didn't mind too much. It meant I had a reason to be out of bed longer, and spend more time with Dart, who had eagerly helped me with the task of cleaning up the ashes. She simply loved being near anything that created heat. Once I was closer to the patch, I dropped the heavy bucket and stood up straight, wiping some of the sweat from my forehead. No one ever talked about how much a bucket of ashes weighed.

Most of the castle was in darkness, but I noticed there was one window lit a few feet away from me. Who could be awake at this time? All of the other servants would have retired for the night, and as far as I was aware, Matron did the same after she'd performed the bed checks. The only person who would still be about is the Duchess herself. But, as the only noble in the castle, surely she'd be in her own rooms? Especially when there was no one to attend on her.

My curiosity piqued, I made my way over to the flower bed under the window, making sure to scratch Dart on the head so she knew I hadn't forgotten about her. With everyone else asleep, there'd be no one to check on how quickly I performed my task, and the only person who would suffer for it taking longer than it should was me and a lack of sleep.

"You need to be more careful," the Duchess' voice rang out from the open window.

She definitely wasn't alone, then. That was odd. No one had arrived at the house since Raynor had departed. Everything had simply gone back to normal. There hadn't been anyone in the kitchens when I'd cleared the grate of ashes, either. Which only deepened the mystery of who she could be talking to.

"Why should I do that?" a man replied.

"The Prince is on to you. He was here these past few days asking questions about you and what kind of troops you had," the Duchess replied.

Ah, then that must be Lord Daryll in there with her, Raynor had said he was suspicious of the local lord. But what did this mean? Was he right to suspect him? And what did the Duchess have to do with all of this? I had more questions than answers, and I had no idea how to get to the bottom of all of them.

"I hope you put him off the scent," Daryll said.

The Duchess laughed. "Of course I did. We have our plan to protect, and at the moment, he clearly believes I'm trustworthy."

"More fool him. He's a bigger idiot than his Father is, if you ask me."

"Tell me about it. He fixated on one of the serving girls and paid no attention to the rest of what was going on in the castle, I didn't even have to steer him away from the storage rooms."

I gasped, then shoved my hand over my mouth in an attempt to keep the sound in. The last thing I needed was to be discovered.

"Can you blame him? You do keep a pretty stable around."

The Duchess snorted. "And why do you think

that is? It's much easier to distract men with pretty girls than anything else."

So that was her motivation in having us all here. She planned to use us for her own advantage. I supposed that wasn't much of a surprise. The Duchess was that kind of person, I'd known that since the beginning. It simply surprised me she was this blatant about it. Even some semblance of decorum would have been better.

"If it worked, then hats off to you. Or to the girl you distracted him with."

She sighed loudly. "Unfortunately, she was the one I least wanted him to spend time with. She normally keeps to herself, and I'd hoped that would be the case this time too."

I frowned as I absentmindedly scratched Dart's head. What could she mean by that? I was like all the other girls, wasn't I?

"When do you think we'll be ready to act?" Daryll asked.

"The ball."

"That soon?" Surprise coloured his tone.

"There is no reason to delay it any longer than that," the Duchess responded. "We have several members of the nobility in place already, plus the weapons and the element of surprise. We should take advantage of that while we can. If we leave it longer, there's always going to be a chance we're discovered."

Much like I was doing now. I didn't even understand everything I was hearing from the two of them, but I knew it was going to change the course of everything. They were plotting against Raynor, despite him being a decent man. And what for? Power? Money? The crown? I wasn't sure. Raynor wasn't the king yet, his Father still held the crown.

I pushed those thoughts aside. The *why* didn't matter. They were planning something, and it was going to spell trouble. And at the ball, no less.

Not wanting to linger any longer under the window, I moved away and back towards where I should be scattering the ashes. I hoped neither of them looked out in my direction, or they might start to worry I'd been listening, and if that was the case...

I shuddered at the thought. I was disposable. Perhaps not to Daryll, who'd see me as a pretty plaything first, but definitely to the Duchess. And if I was trapped by them, then I wouldn't be able to help Raynor in foiling their plans, something I was now certain I had to do.

"We should keep our eyes peeled, Dart," I said to the dragon.

She chittered, and swayed a little more on my shoulder, completely oblivious to what was going on. That was her normal state, unless she was in the dining room tripping me up, of course.

"I have to get to the ball," I added. "It's the only way I can warn him about what's going to happen." I doubted I could get a message to him before that, even if I wanted to.

Briefly, I considered whether or not Dart would be able to fly that far. But no, it was a silly thought. She only had small wings, and wouldn't know the way. Raynor would have no way of knowing she'd been sent from me, either. He had no idea I had a dragon friend, and hadn't seen my writing. It could even be an attempt to get him off the scent of what was going on.

"I don't know how I'm going to do it, but I'll manage," I promised the dragon, who wasn't paying any attention to me and was instead cleaning her wings.

That was what I got for having an animal best friend. She never answered when I needed her to.

CHAPTER NINE

WE STOOD IN A LINE, just like we had when the Prince had first arrived, but judging from the lack of fancy clothing and the other servants not being here, I guessed we weren't going to be entertaining another wealthy visitor. Which made me wonder what the Duchess was up to. It wasn't like her to even talk to one of us, let alone gather us all.

She paced back and forth in front of us, her austere black and white striped gown only serving to make her a more imposing figure than ever. I tried not to let that get to me.

"As some of you may be aware, the royal family are holding a ball tomorrow night," the Duchess said.

All the other girls stood up straighter instantly, probably because they guessed at where this was going. She'd need attendants, it was a sign of power and prestige to have them. And perhaps, while there, they could find a noble to whisk them off their feet and turn them into a mistress. That option wasn't one I ever planned on exploring.

It only took a moment for me to realise I needed to act that way too if I wanted to end up at the ball to warn Raynor about the Duchess' plans.

"I will be taking two of you with me. Though I haven't decided which two yet. Be sure that I will be discussing the choices with Matron and we will be deciding based on which of you have the least capacity to embarrass our great name."

I could almost *feel* the others' desire to start talking amongst themselves about what the ball might be like. No one said a word, though. They wouldn't until the Duchess had walked away and left us all to do our chores. That was the way life at the castle worked, after all.

"That is all. You may return to work." She dismissed us with a wave of her hand.

I bit my lip, trying to consider whether or not I could be as outspoken as I wanted to be. I needed to be at the ball, and the only way to do that was going to be by convincing the Duchess I should be one of the girls she took with her.

I hesitated for a moment too long. The other girls had all disappeared, chattering about the opportunity, but not lingering in the front hall.

"What are you still doing here?" the Duchess demanded.

Oh no. What should I say now? Was it worth pointing out that Raynor took a liking to me? Or would that harm my cause instead of adding to it?

"I'm sorry, Your Grace," I said, dipping into a curtsy. "But I was wondering if there was anything I could do to help with the preparations for the ball. I could start thinking about how to do your hair and..."

She cut me off with a barking laugh. "And you think that by pushing me, you'll convince me it's you I need to take to the ball?"

"Of course not, Your Grace," I lied smoothly. "I'd never presume to influence your decisions."

She narrowed her eyes at me, and I suspected I'd said something wrong without meaning to. Not my best moment, but there wasn't anything I could do about it right now.

"You won't be coming with me," she said flatly.

"But the Prince..."

"My decision is final, and won't change. You won't be accompanying me to the ball, and you were never going to. Put all thoughts of it from your head and focus on your work." She turned on her heels without saying anything else and swept out of the room.

I stared after her. That made no sense. Why was she so against me coming with her? I hadn't done anything wrong that I was aware of. I'd done her extra chores without saying a word against them, the same way I always did. I was one of the best-behaved girls she kept here.

And then I remembered what she'd said to Lord Daryll. I'd been the last girl she'd wanted to catch the eye of the Prince. I had no idea why that was, but I bet it had something to do with why she didn't want to take me to the ball. It was a shame nothing I could do would uncover the reasoning behind that decision.

I sighed loudly. There was nothing else for it, I was going to have to find a different way of getting there. I was reasonably confident when it came to how to ride a horse, I dimly remembered lessons on it from before I arrived at the Duchess' castle. But that didn't mean I could get all the way to the palace on one. I didn't even *know* the way to the palace.

And I couldn't go to a ball dressed in the worn rags of a serving girl, they'd never let me in.

Which meant I needed to find something to

wear, a way to get there, and an excuse to leave the castle, all without raising any suspicions about what I was doing. It sounded challenging, but I'd find a way. I had to warn Raynor that the Duchess was plotting something.

CHAPTER TEN

I STARED INTO THE FLAMES, watching for Dart to move within them. It was still early in the morning, but the Duchess and two of the girls, Nancy and Jill, were about to leave for the ball. If I was going to act, then it would have to be soon so I could follow the tracks of their carriage.

"What am I going to do, Dart?" I asked, giving up on waiting for the dragon to appear. I knew she was there, which meant she could hear me.

To my surprise, she zipped out of the fire and around the kitchen, moving at lightning speed.

I scrambled to my feet, unsure what she was suggesting. It wasn't like her to risk exposure like this. With the Duchess almost ready to depart, the cooks weren't preparing her breakfast and were taking a much-needed rest while they could. It was the same as the rest of us would be doing while Matron wasn't looking.

Dart chirped at me, then left the room, flapping her wings and going out into the main castle.

"This is dangerous," I warned her. "You could get caught."

She landed on one of the bannisters and cocked her head to the side, almost daring me to say more.

I was about to reach her when she launched herself into the air and disappeared up the stairs. I sighed and resisted the urge to roll my eyes. What was she up to? It was impossible to tell. Perhaps I should trust her. She wouldn't lead me into danger.

The memory of me falling while serving the Duchess breakfast flitted through my mind, but I pushed it away. Dart hadn't *meant* for that to happen, I was certain of it. And it wasn't as if it had done any harm. If anything, it had reminded Raynor of my presence and that he wanted to spend time with me.

I glanced around to make sure no one else was watching. Not that it would matter if they were at this point. They'd already have seen Dart, and that was enough to cause problems.

Satisfied we were still alone, I bounded up the stairs after her, intrigued and worried all at the same time. I didn't have long to find a way to the ball, chasing after a dragon for no reason wasn't going to help that.

Dart must have sensed the direction of my thoughts, as she flew back to me, before circling me and chirping loudly.

"I promise, I'm coming with you," I vowed. I shouldn't be so short with her, even in my thoughts. Dart had been my first friend, even before Jill had arrived here, and I shouldn't forget that. She'd stand by me no matter what, and it was only fair I did the same.

She flapped her wings, turning to the left.

I frowned. As far as I was aware, there was nothing more than a wall there. I shook my head. What was the dragon up to?

Dart landed on a tiny rut on the wall and stretched her body upwards, flapping her wings.

"What are you wanting me to do?" I asked her, scanning the wall for clues about what she had in mind. This would teach me to spend so much time with a creature who couldn't speak.

She chirped and pointed her head towards the sconce.

I raised an eyebrow. "You want me to pull on that?"

The dragon nodded.

With a loud sigh, I stepped forward and tugged

on the sconce, not expecting it to do anything. Why would it? We weren't in a children's story. It wasn't going to open up into...

Stone grated against more stone as a door slid open to reveal a dark corridor.

"How do you know about this?" I asked Dart.

Instead of responding, she jumped from her perch and settled herself on my shoulder. Her claws served as a constant reminder she was there, but didn't break my skin. I knew Dart wouldn't do anything to hurt me, even superficially. Our bond was far too strong for that.

I stepped into the corridor, noticing a second sconce just within. That would probably be the one to close the door, then. Testing my theory, I tugged on it.

The grating sound came again, and the two of us were shrouded in the surrounding darkness. Oops. That hadn't gone to plan, I still wanted to be able to see.

I reached out with one of my hands and snapped my fingers, hoping it would be enough to form a small flickering flame. It wouldn't be much to see by, but hopefully, it would be enough to light a torch when I found one. More sconces lined the walls, though the ones I could see at the moment were all empty, I held out hope that one of them wouldn't be.

My tiny flame created eerie shadows along the walls, but I ignored them. I had Dart in case anything went wrong.

"Aha," I said aloud the moment I spotted a torch. I went up onto my toes to fetch it, letting the flame on my fingers flicker out. I didn't want the wrong part of the torch to set on fire while I was getting hold of it.

With the course handle now in my hand, I held it out and tried to bring the small spark I'd been able to produce back. Nothing happened.

"Dart, would you mind?" I asked.

She chittered, and then opened her mouth. A stream of fire jumped from her to the torch. A little too late, I shielded my eyes, but the brightness had already stunned me. It was a good job we were the only two beings down here, otherwise, someone would have been able to take advantage of me right then and there.

"Thanks." I scratched Dart's head. "All right, let's get to the end of this corridor and see what you want me to," I said to her.

I all but ran down the rest of the corridor, eager to get out of the dark and into somewhere that explained this whole journey.

And then it all made sense. The room I stepped into was huge. Light streamed in from the high windows, illuminating the particles dancing through the air. This room wasn't used very much if the amount of undisturbed dust was anything to go by. If the Matron knew about this, she'd have us all in here cleaning every part of the room until it shone.

"What is this place?" I whispered as I set the torch in one of the empty sconces. I didn't want it to go out, I'd need it for my return trip, but with all the light in this place, I didn't need it to see anything else.

Dart jumped from my shoulder and zipped over to one of the racks covered in old cloth.

I frowned, but followed her anyway. If she'd brought me here, then there must have been a reason why, and I should trust that would make sense soon enough.

As soon as she was out of the way, I tugged on the cloth, letting it fall to the floor.

Without me meaning it, a loud gasp escaped. The rack was filled with dresses in all kinds of beautiful fabrics. They'd clearly belonged to a noblewoman before ending up here, and judging from the styles, it hadn't been the Duchess. Did she even know this room existed? And how did Dart know it was here? That was something I wasn't likely to ever get an answer for.

I flicked through the dresses, my gaze lingering

longer than it should on a beautiful grey dress in a silky fabric that felt like heaven to touch. I doubted it was in fashion. But then, I had no way of following what the trends were.

"This one?" I checked with Dart.

The small dragon dipped her head eagerly. She agreed with my choice. That was something, at least. Not that I should be relying on the fashion sense of a dragon.

I pulled it from the rack and held it up against me. It looked as if it would fit. I should try it on, but I was anxious to get away from the castle and ride towards the palace. It wouldn't do if I was late to the ball. The last thing I needed was to miss my chance to warn the Prince about what was coming.

"Come on, Dart," I said. "We'll go saddle one of the horses and be on our way. I'll get dressed once I'm there." I certainly wouldn't be the best-dressed woman there, but I'd still manage to look decent.

She skittered across the floor, drawing my attention to a rack of shoes.

I almost slapped my hand against my forehead. How could I have forgotten I'd need shoes to go with the dress. I crouched down and started sorting through them, dismissing several pairs which were clearly going to be too big or too small. I ended up with three different choices. I couldn't take the same chance as with the dress. If it turned out to be too big, I could do something about it with pins and tucking at the last minute. If the shoes didn't fit, then I'd have to go barefoot to the ball, which didn't sound at all fun.

I pulled my boot off and tried on the first pair. They just about fit, but pinched my toes in a way I was certain would get uncomfortable after mere minutes. Not the best choice.

The second pair were plain white leather. They didn't technically match the dress, but I figured having shoes suitable for a ball was more important than an exact match. The dress was long anyway, and would cover them. I pulled the shoe on only for it to slip straight off. I groaned in frustration. I had to hope the last pair worked, even if they were the ones I was least certain about. They glittered in the sunlight, almost seeming as if they were made of glass. Not the most practical choice for footwear, even if they looked beautiful.

Despite that, I slid my foot inside the shoe. It fit perfectly. Almost as if it had been made for my foot instead of that of whichever noblewoman had left this room behind.

"Glass it is," I told Dart.

She nodded in agreement.

"But we should get going." I pulled my boot back on, then rose to my feet.

A medium-sized bag hung over the rail I'd uncovered. I grabbed it, slipping the shoes and the dress into it to keep them safe. What I'd said to Dart was right, we needed to go. But before we did, I was going to do one last sweep of the room to be sure there wasn't anything else I could use here, and to put the cloth back over the rack. I didn't want any of the dresses to get damaged by the dust or faded by the sunlight if they didn't have to.

Dart leapt from the floor and glided up to my shoulder, settling there once more. I hadn't checked with her, but deep down, I knew she was going to be going to the ball alongside me. It felt right that way. She would be my source of comfort. And she'd help me warn Raynor, even if I had no idea how yet. All I knew was that we were going to succeed, I'd make sure of it.

CHAPTER ELEVEN

I PINNED the last strand of my hair into the fancy up-do I'd created for myself and took a deep breath. This was it. There was no more wasting time. I had to go into the ball and find Raynor in an attempt to stop whatever the Duchess had planned. When put like that, it seemed like a rather simple thing to achieve, but I knew that wasn't going to be the case. It would be a gruelling few hours until the ball wound down around midnight.

And it was only going to get harder with each minute longer it took me to find the Prince.

Dart chirped from beside me.

"I know," I assured her. "I need to get going. But how do I look?" I did a twirl, letting the soft grey fabric swish around my lower legs. In hindsight, perhaps I should have put more thought into which dress I picked, as this one wasn't going to be any good if I had to run anywhere.

It was beautiful, though. With my hair pinned back, the dress gave me an elegant silhouette which would be striking once I reached the ballroom.

Dart whistled, which I assumed was a good thing.

"Time to get going, then?" I asked.

She nodded.

"Why don't you go and try to find the Duchess, I'll go find the Prince?"

She cocked her head to the side in an expression I could only describe as disbelieving.

"I know, I'm sorry. I know she's no fun. But if she recognises me before I get the Prince's protection..."

A tiny ring of smoke escaped from Dart's nose. I was reasonably certain it meant she agreed with me. My theory was proven a moment later when she lifted herself into the air and flew off in the direction of the main hall.

I stowed the bag with my previous dress, cloak, and boots, under one of the wooden seats in the cloakroom. I was lucky no one had come in while I was changing and getting myself ready, or I'd have had some awkward questions to answer. I needed to be back here before midnight to collect my things and set off home before the Duchess did. Unless everything went to plan and I ended up helping the

Prince. Perhaps then, I wouldn't have to return to the castle. I certainly didn't want to if I didn't have to.

The music grew louder the moment I left the cloakroom. I let the upbeat melodies guide me towards the ballroom. If I was here under different circumstances, I might have been excited. This was the first time I'd ever attended a noble function.

If times had been different, perhaps this would still have been my first, but I'd have been introduced to the society by my Father. A young man, perhaps the Prince, would have asked me to dance. I'd have drunk too much champagne, and made myself dizzy with the dancing.

I paused at the thought. Why would the circumstances have been different enough to have allowed that? I was a serving girl, it wasn't likely I'd ever have been able to attend one of these unless it was to hold my mistress' hat. But that wasn't the direction my mind had taken. It was almost as if I *believed* I had a place here. One that wasn't defined as being two steps behind someone.

I shook my head. It was probably the remnants of a dream I'd had once and nothing more than that. I couldn't let a wish distract me from what I was supposed to be doing.

The corridor opened up in front of me, revealing

the grand ballroom of the palace, complete with twirling couples. The dresses were so bright, they almost hurt my eyes. I'd been right about the dress I was wearing not being in fashion. Most of the ladies were wearing jewel tones and skirts that belled out around them, rather than the smokey grey slim fitted gown I'd chosen. At least the flared fabric at the bottom of my dress would make it fit in a little bit better.

I scanned the room, trying to find the Prince, the Duchess, or anyone else I recognised.

A frown marred my face for a moment, before I remembered where I was and replaced it with a smile. Why would I recognise anyone? I only knew four people in this room, and three of them would be in the same place. And that was assuming the Duchess had brought Nancy and Jill in with her. She could very easily have dismissed them as soon as they'd arrived, or have pawned them off on nobles she wanted to gain favour with.

My gaze locked on him, and the breath hitched in my throat.

Raynor.

He looked magnificent in his white military uniform, a small gold circlet on his head, but nothing more. He didn't need anything else to remind everyone he was the Prince, his whole demeanour did that for him.

No one was around him. He stood apart from the festivities, watching them but not giving away his feelings. I wondered if there was a reason for that, or if he was looking for someone in particular.

I had no idea where the Duchess or Lord Daryll were, though I'd never seen the latter in person, so he could be standing right next to me and I wouldn't know. But this was my chance. Raynor was alone, if I could get to him, then I could tell him what I knew and we could work out the rest together.

At least, that was the theory. It would be easier said than done to get over to him through the mass of dancing nobles. There were also the young men without dance partners to contend with. I spied a couple of them watching me already. They weren't causing me any harm, but they could delay me getting to the Prince.

And then I realised none of them mattered, because he'd seen me.

Our eyes locked across the room. He dipped his head in acknowledgement, and I dipped into a curtsy, hoping I didn't give away how much I was shaking while I did it. I wasn't going to have to make my way over to Raynor after all. He'd do the hard work for me.

CHAPTER TWELVE

"You came," Raynor said after he reached me.

"I promised I'd try," I pointed out. "Though if you recognised me from across the room, my disguise isn't very good." I glanced at the floor, concern over the Duchess spotting me twisting in my gut.

"Not at all," he countered. "If this were a masquerade you wouldn't be hidden better."

"That's just flattery."

"I promise, it's not," he assured me. "I'd have known you anywhere, Tanwyn."

"Hmm." I raised an eyebrow at him. He could promise all he wanted, but that didn't mean anything.

My gaze shifted from Raynor to the couples spinning and moving in time with the music.

"Would you like to dance?" he asked.

"I don't know how," I admitted, staring wistfully at the dancers.

"I can teach you as we go," he promised, then leaned in so his lips brushed the shell of my ear. "I'm known as a terrible dancer anyway, you'll only make me look better."

I tried not to let the shiver of anticipation show.

"Fine. But if anyone laughs at me, I'm holding you completely responsible," I joked.

Raynor chuckled. "I'll pay whatever forfeit the lady requests."

"I'm not a lady," I pointed out.

"Maybe I'll make you one."

"Can you do that?" And did I want that? Not that I was going to voice the second question. When it came to royalty, I imagined it didn't much matter what I wanted.

"Not if you don't want me to. Now, shall we?" He gestured to the floor.

I gulped down my nerves.

Raynor held his hand out, and I took it, gladly. I was going to enjoy this, no matter what anyone else said. I might not know how to dance, but I'd do my best.

I placed my hand in his, enjoying the soft touch of skin against skin. Small goosebumps sprang up along my arms. How was he having this effect on me? It hadn't been as pronounced when we were at the Duchess' castle.

People stopped mid-dance as we made our way to the centre of the floor. A thread of guilt thrummed through me, but I pushed it to the side. This had nothing to do with anyone but Raynor and me. It was our moment, and I was going to make the most of it no matter what anyone else said.

He gestured towards the musicians and they stopped playing the song they had been, and began the opening chords of the next.

Was this normal? Could a Prince simply decide he didn't like the song and have them start another? It didn't seem like the best idea to me, but then, what did I know?

Raynor dipped into a deep bow. Instinct told me I should curtsy in return, and I did so, but kept my eyes locked on his. A smile stretched over his handsome face, and I knew I'd done the right thing.

He took one of my hands in his. "Put your other one on my shoulder," he instructed. "I'll place mine on your waist."

I nodded ever so slightly, not wanting anyone else to know I needed this much coaching. I rested my hand on his shoulder, unable to ignore the flex of muscles under his jacket. This was a man in peak health.

"When I step forward, you step back. Move with me," he instructed as the music began in earnest.

"That's it?"

"If you count to four, it might help," he told me.

I started counting in my head, but was surprised to discover his instructions actually seemed to work. It helped that he was guiding me, his sure footwork moving us around the dancefloor, just like I'd seen the other nobles doing.

"You're a natural," he said. "Are you ready to spin?"

"Spin?" I squeaked.

He nodded. "Trust me?"

"Of course."

"Then let go of my shoulder and follow my lead."

I did as he instructed, and he guided me into a graceful spin under his arm. I let out a light laugh, enjoying the freedom the movement brought. I'd never imagined dancing could be like this.

"I thought you said you were a bad dancer," I accused once I was back securely in his arms.

He chuckled. "I'm far from the best. There are lords and ladies here who would put me to shame if they danced with you."

"Then it's a good thing I have no intention of dancing with them," I said without meaning to.

"You're very forward tonight," he observed.

"You're the one who asked me to dance."

"And that now makes you an expert on me?" Amusement shone in his eyes, assuring me I hadn't gone too far in my teasing.

"Only you can answer that," I countered.

He spun me again, and I landed back in his arms.

"Tell me, Tanwyn, was it worth sneaking out of your castle home to come to the ball?" he asked.

My eyes widened at the reminder of what I'd done, and of what I needed to tell him.

"I came here for a reason," I whispered.

"I hoped it was so you could see me." Though his words were teasing, I could tell he was worried about what that could mean.

"That was my first reason," I promised. "But can we go somewhere to talk?"

He nodded and drew me off the dancefloor with practised ease. None of the other dancers even seemed to notice we'd left. That was fine by me, I didn't want to draw attention to us, especially when I hadn't found the Duchess yet. And, even worse, I'd forgotten all about her to a certain extent.

One of the servants offered us glasses of champagne from a silver tray. Raynor passed one to me before getting one for himself and moving us on to the open windows of the ballroom.

"Where are we going?" I asked, my curiosity getting the better of me.

"To the gardens. We'll have some measure of privacy there, but I'm afraid it won't be too much, we'll still have to be careful with what we say."

Relief flooded through me. Not because I'd get to spend more time with him, but because he seemed to have understood the gravity of the situation. I wasn't trying to create problems where none existed, I was simply doing my duty as a citizen of his country. At least, that was what I was going to keep telling myself. In reality, several of my decisions were coming from the place that liked Raynor as a person as well as my Prince.

"Will this be all right?" he asked, indicating a rather cozy looking lovers' seat covered in late summer flowers.

"Yes." Even the thought of being so close to him while we talked had my throat turning dry. I remembered the champagne in my hand and took a sip. I'd only ever had it once before, and that had only been a taste after some had been leftover from one of the Duchess' parties. This was better, though. It was light and bubbly.

Raynor waited for me to take a seat and then sat next to me.

Despite knowing it wasn't proper, I kicked off

the glass-like shoes. They were surprisingly comfortable, but something felt off about wearing another woman's slippers, and I would enjoy having a small amount of time free of them.

"You look beautiful in that dress," Raynor said.

I glanced away, trying to hide the blush stealing over my cheeks. "It's out of fashion," I murmured.

"You think I know what is and isn't stylish?" he checked.

"You have eyes," I pointed out. "And a parade of beautiful noble girls in front of you. I'd think it was hard *not* to notice."

"None of them even compare to you."

I wanted to call him out on that being such a ridiculous thing to say, but I found I couldn't. I enjoyed it too much.

To my surprise, Raynor leaned in and brushed a stray lock of my hair behind my ear. I closed my eyes at the touch, enjoying the intimacy of the moment, which was only increased by the gentle scent of the flowers, and the faint strains of music from the ballroom.

Right here, we were in a world of our own, where no one else mattered.

Raynor's lips touched mine. After a moment of shock, I relaxed into the kiss, letting myself focus on nothing except for the man in front of me. I'd been trying not to think about what this moment might be like. It had seemed so unlikely that a Prince would be interested in a serving girl like me, and I hadn't wanted to push my luck any further than I already had.

We broke apart, both of us breathing heavily and staring at one another. I lifted my fingers to my lips, and touched them. They still tingled from the way he'd kissed me.

"That was everything I imagined it would be," he admitted.

My blush returned. "I was supposed to be warning you, not kissing you," I murmured.

"Warning me?" The haze of emotion and desire left him within moments. "About what?"

"The Duchess," I said. Now that I'd remembered what I was supposed to be doing, rather than letting myself get lost in the romantic haze of the evening, the words came tumbling out. "I overheard her talking to Lord Daryll, that was the lord you thought might be plotting against you, right?" I checked.

He nodded.

"They were talking about the supplies they have and when they're going to make their move. They said it was going to be tonight."

Raynor frowned. "The Duchess said this?"

I nodded. "I was under the window. They didn't realise it..."

"You don't understand, Tanwyn," he started.

Oh no. What was he going to say now? Would he dismiss the warning I'd worked so hard to get to him?

"The Duchess must have been saying all of that to gain Lord Daryll's trust," he said.

Should I protest? I didn't want him to think I was easily swayed, but I knew this was dangerous territory. I could lose Raynor forever if this went wrong.

"Her husband was a huge supporter of my family before he died. His wife can't be plotting against us, it would defile his life's work and leave it in tatters."

"I heard her," I whispered. "She seemed fairly certain." Why didn't he believe me? He had when I'd told him about the girls being used to spy on him, so why didn't he now? I wasn't lying to him.

Tears welled up in my eyes. I held them back, though it got harder with every moment he didn't say anything. How could he be doing this to me? I thought he liked me.

Fool. The word echoed around my head. How could I have ever thought a Prince would be interested? It was probably some kind of sport to him, to see if he could trick a poor girl into thinking she was something more. Perhaps he even had a bet going with someone on the inside.

Raynor sighed loudly, as if he wanted to accept that I was telling the truth, at the same time as needing to deny it for his own peace of mind.

A gong sounded inside. Raynor jumped to his feet, a panicked look on his face. "I'm sorry, Tanwyn, I have to go see to this. It's an important part of the night."

He was gone before I could say anything else. My chance of saving his life along with him.

How could I have gotten this so wrong?

CHAPTER THIRTEEN

I WIPED AWAY the dried tears as I made my way back to the ball. No matter what Raynor said, I believed what I'd heard was true, and I was going to protect him no matter what, even if I had to do it myself and had no idea where to start.

As if she'd sensed my distress, Dart whizzed by me, coming to settle on my shoulder. She chirped and chittered, clearly distressed by something.

"What is it?" I asked, my voice sounding stronger than I'd expected it to. That was something at least. This way, other people didn't need to know I'd had my heartbroken by the first person I'd ever given it to.

Dart jumped off me and flapped her wings frantically. I had no idea what she'd seen, but it was clearly something she didn't like.

"Take me," I whispered.

She turned to the left, back in the direction she'd come from, and away from the party. I frowned. Where could she be taking me? What had she seen? She was supposed to have been finding the Duchess, but how was that possible if we were going in the opposite direction to the ball?

I wanted to ask all my questions aloud, but I knew it was pointless. Dart wouldn't have any answers for me. No, that wasn't true. Dart *did* have answers for me. They were simply communicated in a different way. She couldn't use words, so she showed me instead. It was the main way she told me what she wanted.

Deciding that the best thing I could do was to trust her, I crept along behind her. Every now and again, Dart turned her head around to check I was still there. When she did, I'd nod in her direction and continue moving.

After five minutes of this, we approached what looked like a carriage house. Something wasn't right about it, though. A light flickered in the window, one that I knew would spook whatever horses were inside. I might not know a lot about the creatures, but I'd paid enough attention when the stablehands talked about them to be sure about this.

Dart flew back to me and landed on my shoulder.

This must have been what she was trying to show me. I had very little doubt about what I'd find when I peered through the window, but that didn't mean I shouldn't be careful.

I reached up and scratched the dragon's head in a way of thanks. I didn't want to speak out loud in case we were heard. The last thing either of us wanted was to be discovered. There was no doubt in my mind that the Duchess would kill me if she found me here, and who knew what she'd do to Dart. Probably trap her and then enslave her. That was the Duchess' way.

After listening for a moment to ensure no one was directly on the other side of the window, I popped my head up over the ledge and looked inside. A middle-aged man sat with the Duchess, a sharp knife between the two of them. Judging from his clothing, this could be none other than Lord Daryll.

A small part of me hoped Raynor was looking around the ballroom and noticing that the two of them were missing right now. That would make it easier when I tried to convince him he was in danger again.

"Are you going to do it, or are you expecting me to?" Lord Daryll asked.

I sucked in a breath. I could only guess at what

they were going to do, but I imagined it wasn't going to end well for Raynor. Or the rest of his family, for that matter. I doubted they'd be satisfied with only the Prince out of the way.

Why wasn't Raynor being more careful? I could understand not worrying about his own life so much, but what about his parents? Actually, I had no idea whether or not his Mother was alive. He'd only ever spoke to me of the King.

"I'll do it," the Duchess said, picking up the knife and inspecting it with keen interest. Moonlight glinted from the blade, leaving no doubts about her murderous intent. "I'll be able to get closer to him. I doubt the fool will have forgotten his suspicions about you."

"But you told him I was no threat when he visited you."

At least Daryll's comment confirmed they *were* talking about the Prince. For a moment, I'd hoped they were going to assassinate someone else. Not that killing anyone was acceptable, but it might be easier to warn and save someone who didn't have a royal responsibility.

"Of course I did. But the man is no fool in this. He suspected you for a reason, and I doubt that will have gone away simply because I said a few nice words to him." She paused, a thoughtful look coming over her face. "Besides, we don't know what that girl of mine said to him. Maybe she told him something. He didn't seem the same after the two of them talked."

I squeaked, then crouched down in a hurry, not wanting to be discovered listening in to their conversation. The two of them had a clear disdain for life, and I didn't want to be caught up in it.

Except I already was. In choosing to do whatever I could to save Raynor, I'd put myself in the thick of their plot.

"We need to cut them off from the palace," I whispered to Dart.

She made an odd noise that I assumed was approval.

"Maybe with a fire?"

Her eyes lit up. She was always going to choose fire over every other option.

I didn't wait for the two plotters to leave the carriage house. If I wanted to set a fire they wouldn't be able to pass, then it would need some time to grow between me setting it and them getting up to go back to the ball.

"Did you see anything that would burn well?" I asked Dart.

She nodded, then flapped her wings, soaring off into the night just slow enough for me to be able to follow. I'd have to make her a nice fire of her own once all of this was over, a way to treat her and thank her for all the things she'd done to help me over the years.

I found Dart perched on top of an old dry hay bail. A slow grin spread over my face. This would be perfect for what I needed.

Being careful not to ruin my dress, I pushed on the bail so it rolled into the path between the carriage house and the palace. I wasn't naive enough to think it'd be impossible to get around the blaze, but the Duchess was dressed for a party, not for an assassination, she couldn't afford to get too dirty, or it would raise questions about what she'd been up to. Which would also suit my purposes. Anything that could stop her from fulfilling her goal.

"You go be the lookout," I instructed Dart.

She glanced longingly at the hay bail, but I waved her away. Her eyesight was better, and she'd spot them coming far quicker than I would. Besides, the hay was dry, I had no reason to think it wouldn't light with one of the simple sparks I could produce.

The moment she was gone, I clicked my fingers.

Nothing happened.

"Come on," I whispered, trying to encourage the fire inside me.

I clicked them again. This time, the tiniest of

sparks drifted away from my fingers. That wasn't good enough, though. I needed more than that.

Again.

Another spark.

"Please," I whispered frantically.

I shouldn't have sent Dart to go look out after all. She'd have been able to set this on fire in a second.

I clicked another time. This time, a small flame licked up from the tips of my fingers. I smiled, satisfied that I'd finally been able to produce it. Now all I needed to do was use it to light the bail on fire.

Holding the flame next to the dry hay, I counted to ten, waiting for it to catch alight.

Nothing happened.

"Come on..."

Dart came back into view, flapping frantically.

"It won't light," I hissed at her.

She glanced over her tiny shoulder. The others couldn't be far behind.

"Try once?" I asked, letting the flame on my fingers drift away in the breeze.

Dart didn't do anything to acknowledge she'd heard me. Instead, she opened her mouth and let forth a spew of fire. It hit the bail, but still, nothing happened.

"It must be spelled," I whispered to her. It was the only thing that made sense. Though I couldn't blame the royal stablehands for taking that precaution. A fire would spook the horses and potentially lead to equine death, something they'd want to avoid at all costs.

The soft footfalls of the Duchess and Lord Daryll sounded as they approached.

I exchanged a worried glance with Dart. This was going to be dangerous. If they caught me here, then it would be game over. I was the only person who knew they were planning to hurt Raynor, and if they could stop me from doing anything about it, then they'd be free to go ahead with the plan.

With no other option, I flattened myself against the side of the hay bail they couldn't see.

"What is that doing here?" the Duchess asked with disdain.

"Maybe it's feeding time?" Lord Daryll responded.

I almost rolled my eyes. What did the Duchess see in him as far as a plotting partner went? He didn't seem like the brightest spark.

"Was it here when you came down from the ball?" she asked.

"I'm not sure," he responded.

"You're useless. Check the ground is dry, I don't want to ruin my gown."

"Your gown?" Daryll sounded outraged. "You're thinking about your gown right now?"

"No, I'm thinking about not getting caught," she countered. "All of the places I could ruin a gown are out of bounds to ball goers. Don't you think it would arouse suspicion if I returned with it destroyed?"

Daryll muttered something I couldn't hear over the pounding beat of my heart. Once I knew which side of the bail he was going to check, I could disappear around the opposite side. It wasn't the best strategy, but it was one I hoped would keep me and Dart safe.

His footsteps sounded from the right. "It's dry," he announced.

I almost sighed with relief when the rustling of the Duchess' dress indicated she'd followed in the same direction.

Taking the chance I had, I disappeared around the left hand side of the bail, keeping the two of us out of sight from the woman who ruled my life.

Now, I had to go back to the ball and foil the plot itself.

CHAPTER FOURTEEN

THE BALL WAS STILL in full swing, though it was easy to see that the people in the room had gotten drunker. Probably due to the free-flowing champagne. I suspected it took more than the one glass I'd had myself, though saying that, I'd had the Duchess' plot to sober me up.

My heart pounded in my chest as I searched the room for Raynor. Maybe he'd retired for the evening and was safely behind doors with guards. Even as I thought it, I knew that wasn't going to be the case. Whatever he'd left me to go do, he hadn't been too angry, and I didn't believe he'd leave the ball without at least trying to say goodbye.

"You're going to have to hide in my dress while we're in there," I told Dart. "No one else has a dragon with them."

She chittered as if insulted at the mere suggestion.

"How about next time, I wear a hat. You can pretend to be a decoration on it."

She stared at me for a moment, then nodded her head.

Despite the seriousness of the situation, I found myself smiling. She was such a breath of fresh air in the world I'd found myself in. I wasn't sure what I'd ever do without her. She might have protested about hiding in my dress, but she scampered down and attached herself to one of the fluffy parts at the bottom. It was a good thing she was so small, otherwise, the weight of her might have weighed me down as I reentered the ballroom.

Even so, there wouldn't be any more dancing for me without her disappearing first. The last thing I wanted was for her to end up caught in my dress as I swirled. What if somebody stood on her?

I shook my head. There was no point worrying over Dart right now, she was safe, and even if she wasn't, she was more than capable of looking after herself, she didn't need me to do it for her.

Raynor caught my eye and gave me a small half-wave.

Relief crashed through me. He wasn't angry with

me. I couldn't believe how worried I'd been about that. It seemed silly now, but he was special, and I didn't want to ruin any chance I had with him.

I skirted the edge of the room in an attempt to get closer to him. Hopefully, no one would think that was odd, especially after they'd seen us dancing earlier. As I did so, I scanned the room for any signs of the Duchess and Lord Daryll. They should have arrived before me, and yet they were nowhere to be seen.

Which meant that the first thing I needed to do was to try and warn Raynor again. Perhaps he'd believe me now he had some time to think about it. If not, maybe I'd be able to get him to agree to a search of the Duchess, which would bring up the knife. I didn't think that would be enough to convict her of treason, but as far as I knew, it was against the law to have a weapon while attending a royal ball.

Wait, that was another thing I had no way of knowing. What was happening to me? In some ways, it was almost as if I knew this world already. Which made no sense. I'd never been a part of it, even tangentially.

A hand clasped around my upper arm. I pulled against whoever it was, knowing they weren't a friend of mine. I didn't like anyone touching me without permission, the only potential exception being Raynor, but I could see him in front of me, and knew it wasn't him holding onto me so tightly.

"What do you think you're doing?" a familiar voice growled.

I turned to find Lord Daryll looking at me with contempt in his eyes.

"I'm sorry, do I know you?" I asked, my voice a jittery mess. Technically, even though I knew who he was, he had no idea about that. We'd never met or even seen each other across a room.

"I think you do," he growled. "You see, you forgot one thing when you came waltzing into this ballroom with bad intentions."

I did? Part of me wanted to ask what he thought I'd forgotten, but I thought better of it. If I didn't antagonise him, then perhaps he'd let me go.

"Did you forget that two of your little friends are here tonight?" He pointed to the opposite side of the room where Nancy and Jill were standing looking very out of place, as well as uncomfortable.

"I don't know them, you've got the wrong person," I lied.

He laughed bitterly. "You're just like your Father," he mused. "He didn't know when it was better to stay out of things either. That's what got him dead."

My blood felt like it turned to ice in my veins. What did he know about my Father? No. I shouldn't fall for his trap. I was an orphan, there was nothing to know about the man who sired me.

I pulled my attention away from my own predicament to check on Raynor. My eyes widened as I realised the Duchess was making her approach, though she kept getting waylaid by other nobles who wanted a piece of her time. I supposed in some ways, that was what she got for being one of the highest-ranking people in the land.

Right now, she was also the deadliest. Would any of the people around Raynor be able to protect him when she went in for the strike?

"It looks like your Prince is looking for you," Daryll sneered, squeezing harder on my arm. "Perhaps later, you'll be able to show me how you entrapped him."

"I didn't do anything," I responded, dropping the pretence of not knowing what was going on. It was clear he wouldn't believe a word I said, so it was better to simply play along with whatever he believed to be the case.

He chuckled darkly. "I think you're as innocent as I am." His grip tightened again. "Wave to your Prince, pretend everything is all right."

The urge to go against his instructions was almost too strong to ignore. I had to trust that Raynor would be alarmed about me merely spending time with the man he suspected of plotting against his family and be on alert as a result. I couldn't think of any other signal to use.

I half-waved at Raynor when his eyes scoured over me.

He frowned, his eyes flitting between me and Daryll. I hoped he understood and didn't think I was working with the man to bring him down. That would be worse than the Duchess parting us.

"I believe our dear Duchess is almost at her target," Daryll taunted.

I struggled against him, but he was stronger and in a better position than I was. Plus, he didn't have another living creature hiding in his outfit to look out for. My eyes widened.

"Dart." I didn't give her any other instructions, I couldn't without giving both of us away. The Duchess wouldn't be able to hear us from this distance, but I didn't want to risk Daryll giving her some kind of signal.

The tiny dragon left my dress in a flurry of wings, making herself as streamlined as possible in order to get across the ballroom in as little time as possible.

"What did you do?" Daryll asked, pulling me around so he was facing me.

I tried to smile smugly, but I wasn't sure it worked. The Duchess and Raynor were out of my line of sight now, and it was hard to feel anything other than concern while I couldn't see them.

Daryll's face said it all though. Something bad was happening.

I took the opportunity his distraction caused and yanked my arm down, breaking his hold on me. I stumbled back, not turning around yet. I couldn't while he was still so close. He'd gotten hold of me once, it wouldn't happen again.

He reached out to grab for me, yanking on a handful of dress. My heart almost broke as a terrible ripping sound filled the air. I pushed past it, though. What was a dress compared to someone's life? One could be replaced, the other never could.

I reached out and pushed him away, taking him by surprise. He fell to the floor with a sickening thunk.

Not wanting to waste any time, I picked up the skirts of my dress and slipped off my shoes, I wasn't able to move particularly quickly while wearing them, and speed was of the essence right now.

I had no idea what Dart had done to the Duchess, but she was using one of the serving boys to pull her up from the floor. Dart had probably gone for her signature tripping move, then. A surge of affection for the tiny dragon filled me. She'd understood my desires perfectly.

"Raynor," I breathed out, relieved he was all right.

"What's going on?" he asked, taking in my dishevelled appearance. I was almost certain my hair had fallen out, and added to the rips in my dress and the unladylike way I was acting, I suspected it looked like quite a sight.

"Lord Daryll attacked me." Not technically a lie. But Raynor must have missed what had happened with the commotion going on as the Duchess fell. Everything was going according to plan. Ish.

The woman was on her feet now, and glowering at me. I tried not to cower under her glare, but it was more difficult than I expected. She was a formidable woman at the best of times, and right now, she was trying to be worse than that.

Would she still try to attack the Prince? Surely she had to see how futile that was? She'd be crazy to try it.

As she grew closer, it became clear that she wasn't in her right frame of mind. The soft glint of metal called attention to the knife clutched in her left hand as she approached Raynor and me.

Without any clue of what else to do, I pushed him

back and stood between him and the Duchess. My whole body shook with fear as she lashed out.

One of the guards was quicker, knocking the knife from her hand and sending it skittering across the floor. She was faster than he was to respond, though, and had him on the floor with a firm backhand.

It didn't do anything for my confidence.

"Surrender," I said loudly. A lot of the other guests had stopped celebrating and were now paying attention to the altercation between the Duchess and their Prince. "You won't escape the palace if you try to take his life." My heart pounded in my throat, and I wanted to throw up from the stress of facing down the woman who'd suppressed me for most of my life.

"Stand aside, useless girl," she sneered.

"No." The word almost vibrated with power. I wasn't sure what Raynor was doing behind me, but I hoped he wasn't going to be insulted by me stepping in for him. It wasn't that I thought he was incapable, I just wanted him to be safe. In this situation, my life is expendable, his isn't.

"You were worthless the day I acquired you, and you're even more worthless now," she half-shouted, her face contorted in a way I'd never seen before. This woman was nothing like the steady and cold Duchess I'd come to know.

I kept my cool, knowing it was the only way of getting out of this alive.

The Duchess lurched forward, grabbing hold of my dress and ripping it some more. I wanted to flush at the thought of everyone seeing my exposed skin, but now wasn't the time for that. I had other things to focus on.

My fingers began to tingle. I frowned. It was an odd sensation, one I'd only ever felt when I tried to call the sparks to my hands. I gave in to the sensation, and thin whips of fire leapt from my hands. My eyes widened, but I didn't let my disbelief distract me.

The Duchess didn't think that far ahead, and jumped back in shock. I sent the tendrils out, able to control them better than I expected. They wrapped around her waist, and then tied her hands, creating a pair of fiery handcuffs she wouldn't be getting out of without my say so.

Satisfied she was under control, I turned to Raynor. "There's a storage room in her castle somewhere that has all the evidence you need to convict her, and potentially Lord Daryll." Though I imagined the two of them would turn on one another the moment they could, particularly if they thought it would get themselves out of trouble.

I didn't wait for Raynor to say anything. I

couldn't. I had to find Dart, and then consider what I'd discover about myself tonight. The fiery bonds were still on the Duchess, but I didn't need to do anything to control them any longer. That was almost scarier than any of the other things I'd been able to do.

CHAPTER FIFTEEN

THE LOVE SEAT we'd sat in earlier had seemed like as good a place as any to contemplate my fate. I scratched Dart's head absentmindedly. The exhausted dragon had curled up in my lap after all the excitement and didn't seem like she was going to move any time soon. So I sat there, giving her the attention she needed and trying not to think.

I'd unpinned my hair, but that didn't even start to deal with the tears in the fabric of my dress, nor did it help the shoes I'd lost. I suspected that if I went back inside the palace, I'd be able to find my shoes, and would be given something to cover the ripped dress, but I wasn't ready. The Duchess and Daryll were no doubt gone, hidden away in the dungeons and treated to nothing more than hard bread and gruel.

I snorted at the thought. After years of suffering through the Duchess' offcuts, it almost felt like fate that she'd be forced to eat much worse. But I shouldn't laugh at her misfortune, even if she had brought it on herself.

"Is anyone sitting here?" Raynor asked.

I glanced up sharply, not having expected him to come find me at all. After what he'd seen me do, and after I'd ruined his ball, the last thing I expected was for him to show me any kindness. I didn't deserve it.

"No." The word slipped out before I'd properly thought it through.

The seat wasn't designed to give two people any personal space once they were sat on it together, hence the name. But it was torture to feel my knee brush against his and know that nothing could come of it.

"Who is this?" he asked, gesturing towards Dart.

Ah. Good. A neutral topic. I could talk about Dart until the end of the world and it would never get personal.

"She's called Dart. She's my best friend."

At the sound of her name, the dragon lifted her head. She cocked it to the side, studying the newcomer. She chirped at him, but then curled back up.

"I'm sorry, she's done a lot more flying than

normal," I explained. "I've never seen her this tired before." It was a strange sight now I thought about it. Dart was always so full of energy that seeing her still would have been alarming if I hadn't known the reason why.

"What year were you born?" Raynor blurted.

"What?" The word slipped out before I'd thought about it. "I'm not sure, I've never celebrated my birthday. I think I'm eighteen, though."

He nodded. "That makes sense." He handed me a scroll of parchment.

I stopped stroking Dart so I could take it from him. Slowly, I unfurled it.

"It's a family tree," I said.

He nodded. "I think it's your family tree." He pointed to the bottom.

Tanwyn.

"I don't understand."

"You're the Duchess' step-daughter," he said patiently. "You said you assumed you were the daughter of a minor noble, right?"

"Mmhmm."

"You were almost right. This is Duke Floren, he was my Father's chief advisor. He had a daughter about my age that I remembered playing with as a child. And then, she just disappeared. It wasn't long after the Duke had remarried. He was dead within a year, too. We always assumed the same thing had happened to his daughter, but..."

"Oh." I blinked a couple of times, unsure what to make of that. I did have vague memories of my time before the Duchess, and they'd all suggested I'd been noble at some point in my life. Plus, I'd seemed to understand some of the rules and etiquette surrounding the balls.

But not all of it.

"You can decide what you want to do with the information," he said. "If you want to make it completely go away, then you can. If you want to inherit your Father's lands and titles, then you can."

"What happens to them if I don't?" I asked.

"They'll be forfeit to the crown when the Duchess is put in front of a jury of her peers," he admitted. "I'd rather not have that happen."

I bit my lip to stop myself from saying anything I was going to regret. "Do you mind if I think about it?"

"Of course. Take as long as you need. We can delay the Duchess' trial for as long as we need to. I'm sure some time in the dungeons will do her good."

I snorted. "I don't think she knows the meaning of the word."

"No, I suspect not."

An uncomfortable silence began to grow between the two of us.

"I need to say thank you," he whispered. "Without you, I'd probably be dead."

"Your guards would have stepped in," I pointed out.

He shook his head. "But they didn't. They could have done something at any point, but not one of them thought to lift a finger."

"They were probably in shock," I suggested. "There aren't many people who would think about harming a Prince like that."

"I suppose that is true. Though we're going to have to do a proper investigation into them all in case one or more of them were in league with the Duchess the entire time."

I nodded. That made sense. While the Duchess and Lord Daryll were the only two people involved that I knew about, there was no doubt in my mind that they weren't the only ones involved. There had to be others, or their plot wouldn't have gotten them anywhere.

Raynor reached out and brushed a stray strand of hair behind my ear, the same way he had done earlier.

Despite myself, I flinched away. How could he touch me? He'd seen what had happened in the ballroom, how could he bear to touch me? Magic like that wasn't normal, and using it without training was even less so.

"I'm sorry, I can't." I rose to my feet, being careful to carry Dart in my arms so she didn't fall. The last thing she deserved was to be dropped on the floor, especially when she'd worked so hard to protect me and the Prince.

"Tanwyn..."

I opened my mouth to say something else, but the words froze on my tongue. There wasn't anything left. Everything was over. Ruined. And I had the Duchess to thank for that.

"I'm sorry," I repeated, before running off in the direction of the stables. The only place I could think of being right now was the castle with all the other girls. At least they didn't know the truth about me. I'd be safe there.

CHAPTER SIXTEEN

No one knew the truth about me. Not yet. Except for Dart, but she wasn't about to tell anyone. But all it did was make me question *why* I hadn't known any of this before. If I was the daughter of the Duke that used to own this castle, then why didn't I have any memories of it?

Except, that wasn't true. Now I was walking through the rooms of the castle with the knowledge of who I might be, memories were starting to return.

This room held an echo of Father sitting with me by the fire and presenting me with a dragon egg. I'd only been five, but I hadn't believed him when he'd told me what it was. I supposed that at least explained where Dart had come from. We'd always been tied together, and this only went to prove it.

"Tanwyn?" Jill said nervously from the door.

I pushed away my thoughts and turned to face her. She and Nancy had arrived back at the castle the day after me, and neither of them had put themselves in my presence since. Which made sense. No doubt they were scared about what I would do to them, even if I could never use magic against anyone who I didn't think deserved it.

"Is everything all right?" I asked. I set down the book I'd been pretending to read and scratched Dart under the chin. She was curled up on my lap, a position she'd started to take more and more in the past few days as things around the castle fell apart. Without the Duchess' firm grip, everyone was at odds, not understanding what they should be doing with their time. They were waiting for someone to take charge, and while I knew it was probably supposed to be me who did that, I couldn't bring myself to yet.

"There's a visitor asking for you."

I frowned. Who could be calling on me? "I can go meet them."

She shook her head. "They said not to make you do that. They'd come to you."

"All right, then." I glanced around the room, hoping there wasn't anything particularly out of place. "Will you show them here, please?" That seemed like the best option, given the circumstances.

"Of course." She started to dip into a curtsy, then stopped, realising it was only me in the room. "I'm sorry," she whispered.

I frowned. "For what?"

"We told Lord Daryll we saw you and..."

I shrugged. "It doesn't matter," I promised her. "What's done is done, and I know you didn't do it to hurt me."

She eyed me suspiciously, probably trying to work out if I was telling the truth or not. My heart cracked. I might finally have some answers about my past, but I didn't about the others. But I needed to set them free to learn.

"I'm still sorry."

"I know. But I'd have done the same thing," I pointed out. "We all would have."

"I suppose..." Jill still didn't look particularly comfortable with the situation, but I knew it would only take time. She was the one who needed to come to terms with it.

"After the visitor is gone, will you ask everyone to gather together? There's something I need to tell them."

It was her turn to frown. "What can you say?"

"That I'm the Duchess now, and that they're free to stay or go as they please, but the past rules of the household will no longer apply either way. There'll be wages, but I haven't worked any of that out yet." Huh. Perhaps I was ready to accept my alternate identity.

"Do you have the authority to do that?"

I held back a chuckle. She'd never have asked the Duchess that, but I didn't mind. It was going to take some getting used to for everyone. Myself included.

"I do."

She nodded, then left the room, hopefully to do what I'd asked of her. I straightened my skirts and made sure I was sitting properly. I had no idea who was calling on me. Perhaps it was someone for the ex-Duchess who hadn't heard she was stuck in the palace dungeon yet. No. That wasn't going to be the case. If they'd asked for her, Jill would have checked to say what we should be telling them.

A knock sounded on the door, followed by it opening.

"Your visitor," Jill said, dipping into a real curtsy now.

I sucked in a shocked breath as Raynor entered the room.

"I'll fetch the two of you some tea," Jill said quickly. "I think the cooks have been baking too. I'll see if they have some tarts to spare."

The door clicked shut behind her, leaving the two of us alone.

"That was certainly different to the last time I was here," he observed. "Have you taken to your new role as Duchess well?" He sat in the chair opposite me, without being asked. I supposed there wasn't much room for propriety between us now.

"I haven't taken it at all, yet," I responded. "But once you leave, I will be."

"And turfing them all out onto the street so you can be alone in this big drafty castle?"

"Of course not," I protested. "If they want to stay here, then they can."

"That's very generous of you."

Dart woke up at the sound of his voice and craned her neck in his direction before pawing on the soft fabric of my gown. I'd been back to the secret dress room to find some nicer things to wear. If what Raynor had told me was true, then the dresses belonged to my ancestors anyway. Potentially even my Mother, which meant I had every right to wear them.

"Not generous. They don't deserve to be left without a home simply because the Duchess did something bad," I pointed out.

"You'll make a great ruler, one day," he observed wistfully.

"Of this tiny bit of land, no doubt."

"Your Duchy is actually rather large. If you have a

map, I can point it out to you later, if you want
me to."

I thought about it for a moment.

"I'd like that."

"So, you're not going to pull away from me this
time?"

I studied him. Was that why he was here? Did he
want me to tell him he had nothing to worry about
and I wasn't repulsed by him?

"That didn't have anything to do with you," I
promised.

"I know." He rubbed a hand over his face. "When
Mother asked if she could meet the woman who
saved my life, I had to tell her I'd done something to
make you run away. She got the full rundown of
events from me, then called me a lovesick fool and
explained that pulling away had nothing to do with
me, and was your way of worrying that I wouldn't
see you the same after the fire ropes." A loving grin
spread over his face as he talked about his Mother.
At least I now knew she was still around. It
answered one of the questions I had about him.

"She sounds like a wise woman."

"She is," he acknowledged. "Because she also told
me that if I came to visit after a few days, you'd be
willing to talk to me. And perhaps willing to accept a
gift."

"I guess that depends on the gift," I countered.

He chuckled. "It's more returning something." He picked up the box he'd brought into the room with him and handed it to me.

I moved Dart off my lap so I could lean forward and take it from him, placing her on the chair next to me. She barely moved, even to tell me off for the moving. My fingers brushed against Raynor's as I took the box from him, sending tingles throughout my entire body.

It wasn't a very heavy box, which only confused me about the size. Shouldn't it be smaller if it was something so light? Unable to put aside my curiosity, I lifted the lid.

Laughter bubbled out of me. "My shoes."

"Well, yes. I thought you might want them back." Raynor glanced down, clearly embarrassed by the situation. "Though there is a difference. I had one of the Mages at court enchant them so they'll break any memory spell put over you when you put them on."

My eyes widened. "A memory spell?"

"You don't seem to have any memories of your Father, if I'm guessing right?"

I swallowed and nodded.

"But you were seven or eight the last time anyone saw you. There should be memories there. Which means that the Duchess placed some kind of spell on you. These will break it."

My eyes began to water, but I pushed the tears back. Now wasn't the time to be getting all emotional. "Thank you, you have no idea what that means to me."

"I'd also like to invite you to the palace along with the other nobles who live there," he said. "The Mages can teach you how to control your fire magic better, and perhaps we can court one another."

I sucked in a breath. He wanted to court me? Our kiss had been perfect, but then he'd seen me do crazy things with magic. Surely, he wouldn't want anything to do with me now.

"You don't have to accept it now," he said softly. "The offer will always be open."

"Can Dart come?" I blurted. Now I realised I could be out in the open with her, I wasn't ready to give her up.

He frowned, not having expected that line of questioning. "Of course. Many of the nobles bring pets, though I don't think many of them have dragons. You'll be the envy of the court with her."

"I'm sure that'd be true even if everyone had dragons."

"You have a point." He paused for a moment. "Does that mean you accept?"

I nodded. "I have to settle some things here first, but after that, I will return to the palace with you."

"And you'll let me court you?"

"Yes," I whispered, hardly believing what I was saying. "I'd like nothing better."

EPILOGUE

One Year Later...

"Dart, you can't stay there," I scolded as the small dragon tried to hide in my bouquet. "You realise I'll be throwing it in the air at one point?"

She chuffed, but left the flowers alone anyway.

"You can ride on my shoulder?" I suggested. Everyone was used to my dragon companion by now, and most people would find it odd if I didn't have her with me on my wedding day.

She didn't make any noise, but jumped into the air and soared towards me, landing on my shoulder. At least I'd had the foresight to tell the royal seamstresses not to put any delicate lace on my shoulders.

Dart was good at not causing me any harm, but fabric was another matter.

"We're ready for you," one of the officials told me.

I smiled. This was it. I was going to marry the man who'd changed my life, even if it had been an accident. Once we'd started courting, it had become evident this was going to be the path we'd follow. And I hadn't looked back.

The music began to play, cueing me that it was my time to walk down the centre of the aisle. I took a steadying breath. Even if I wasn't nervous about what the future held, there were a lot of eyes on me today. And I supposed there would be for the rest of my life. When the day was over, I'd be a Princess. When Raynor became King, I'd be his Queen. This was certainly not the way I thought my life would go when I woke up the day he arrived at the Duchess' castle.

I nodded to the people in the crowd as I passed. Some of them I knew, most I didn't. There were a few ladies who openly despised me for having caught the eye of the Prince. I had to keep my eyes on them or they'd try and steal my place. Not that I worried Raynor would stray. He wouldn't. But his Court was full of men and women who would kill for an advantage, the Duchess and Lord Daryll had been proof of that.

A pang of sadness travelled through me at the thought. My Father should be here today, walking me down the aisle to marry the son of his greatest friend. But that wasn't going to be the case. The Matron had told me the Duchess made my Father disappeared, which I assumed meant she'd killed him, but I wasn't sure about that. If I'd been able to punish the woman all over again, then I would. But her sentence had been carried out the day I'd returned to the palace with Raynor. A life in prison with no chance of escape. And terrible meals, I'd been assured. Lord Daryll hadn't been so lucky, and had paid the price for their plot with his life.

I pushed those thoughts aside. I was a bride on her wedding day, I shouldn't be thinking about such morbid things. Not with a life full of happiness in front of me.

I nodded to Jill and Nancy as I passed them. Jill had taken over the running of the castle in my absence, after I'd fired the Matron, and it was seeing a bountiful harvest under her rule. Nancy had left when I'd given her the option, and had become a businesswoman of some kind. They were both doing well for themselves if the quality of their clothing was anything to go by.

Dart chittered in excitement as Raynor stepped forward. I hadn't been able to see him through the crowd, but now I did, my heart skipped a beat. He was as handsome as ever in his military uniform.

A smile spread over his face, and he gave me a little wave.

I made the same gesture back, enjoying the familiarity with which we could communicate now. It wasn't proper of us to do this, but no one would care. We were two people in love, and that was something to be celebrated over anything.

He didn't wait for me to come to him. Instead, he strode down the aisle and took one of my hands in his. Dart jumped from her perch and flapped her wings, diving around us and making all kinds of happy sounds. She was so easily pleased sometimes. But I loved that.

"You look beautiful," he whispered.

"You don't look so bad yourself," I teased.

He tugged me to him, and despite the fact I knew this went against protocol, I went with him.

His lips pressed against mine in a deep kiss. I relaxed into it, enjoying the feel of him by me. I was dimly aware of the gasps and shock of the people around us, but they could wait.

We broke apart, broad grins on our faces.

"I'm sorry, I couldn't wait all the way through the ceremony to do that," he admitted.

I laughed lightly. "It's a good job you're royalty,

you wouldn't be able to get away with anything otherwise."

A small smirk lifted the side of his mouth. "Then we'll be eternally grateful that's the case." He held out his arm for me. "Would you like to get married now, Duchess?"

"You won't be calling me that for much longer," I pointed out.

Dart landed back on my shoulder. She must have sensed that we were done with our kiss.

"No, I'll be calling you wife," he teased.

"And I can't wait."

We stood before the altar, ready to say our vows and begin our happily ever after.

* * *

The End

* * *

Thank you for reading *Tainted Ashes*, I hope you enjoyed it! If you want more from the Untold Tales series, the next book is *Braided Silver*, a retelling of Rapunzel: http://books2read.com/braidedsilver

completed series)

- Grimalkin Academy: Kittens Series (paranormal academy, completed series)
- Grimalkin Academy: Catacombs Trilogy (paranormal academy, completed series)
- City Of Blood Trilogy (urban fantasy)
- Grimalkin Academy: Stakes Trilogy (paranormal academy)
- The Harpy Bounty Hunter Trilogy (urban fantasy)
- Bite Of The Past (paranormal romance)
- Sabre Woods Academy (paranormal academy)
- The Shadow Seer Association (urban fantasy)

Books in the Forgotten Gods World

- The Queen of Gods Trilogy (paranormal/mythology romance)
- Forgotten Gods Series (paranormal/mythology romance, completed series)

The Grimm World

- Grimm Academy Series (fairy tale

academy)
- Fate Of The Crown Duology (Arthurian Academy)
- Once Upon An Academy Series (Fairy Tale Academy)

Other Series

- Untold Tales Series (urban fantasy fairy tales)
- The Dragon Duels Trilogy (urban fantasy dystopia)
- ME Contemporary Standalones (contemporary romance)
- Standalones
- Seven Wardens, co-written with Skye MacKinnon (paranormal/fantasy romance, completed series)
- The Firehouse Feline, co-written with Lacey Carter Andersen & L.A. Boruff (paranormal/urban fantasy romance)
- Kingdom Of Fairytales Snow White, co-written with J.A. Armitage (fantasy fairy tale)

Twin Souls Universe

- Twin Souls Trilogy, co-written with Arizona Tape (paranormal romance, completed series)
- Dragon Soul Series, co-written with Arizona Tape (paranormal romance, completed series)
- The Renegade Dragons Trilogy, co-written with Arizona Tape (paranormal romance, completed series)
- The Vampire Detective Trilogy, co-written with Arizona Tape (urban fantasy mystery, completed series)
- Amethyst's Wand Shop Mysteries Series, co-written with Arizona Tape (urban fantasy)

Mountain Shifters Universe

- Valentine Pride Trilogy, co-written with L.A. Boruff (paranormal shifter romance, completed series)
- Magic and Metaphysics Academy Trilogy, co-written with L.A. Boruff (paranormal academy, completed series)
- Mountain Shifters Standalones, co-written with L.A. Boruff (paranormal romance)

Audiobooks: www.authorlauragreenwood.co.
uk/p/audio.html

ABOUT THE AUTHOR

Laura is a USA Today Bestselling Author of paranormal and fantasy romance. When she's not writing, she can be found drinking ridiculous amounts of tea, trying to resist French Macaroons, and watching the Pitch Perfect trilogy for the hundredth time (at least!)

FOLLOW THE AUTHOR

- Website: www.authorlauragreenwood. co.uk
- Mailing List: www. authorlauragreenwood.co.uk/p/mailing-list-sign-up.html
- Facebook Group: http://facebook.com/ groups/theparanormalcouncil
- Facebook Page: http:// facebook.com/authorlauragreenwood
- Bookbub: www.bookbub.com/authors/ laura-greenwood

- Instagram: www.
  instagram.com/authorlauragreenwood
- Twitter: www.twitter.com/lauramg_tdir